BROADS, DON'T SCARE EASY

THE CLASSIC HANK JANSON

The first original Hank Janson book appeared in 1946, and the last in 1971. However, the classic era on which we are focusing in the Telos reissue series lasted from 1946 to 1953. The following is a checklist of those books, which were subdivided into five main series and a number of 'specials'.

PRE-SERIES BOOKS
When Dames Get Tough (1946)
Scarred Faces (1947)

SERIES ONE
1) This Woman Is Death (1948)
2) Lady, Mind That Corpse (1948)
3) Gun Moll For Hire (1948)
4) No Regrets For Clara (194)
5) Smart Girls Don't Talk (1949)
6) Lilies For My Lovely (1949)
7) Blonde On The Spot (1949)
8) Honey, Take My Gun (1949)
9) Sweetheart, Here's Your Grave (1949)
10) Gunsmoke In Her Eyes (1949)
11) Angel, Shoot To Kill (1949)
12) Slay-Ride For Cutie (1949)

SERIES TWO
13) Sister, Don't Hate Me (1949)
14) Some Look Better Dead (1950)
15) Sweetie, Hold Me Tight (1950)
16) Torment For Trixie (1950)
17) Don't Dare Me, Sugar (1950)
18) The Lady Has A Scar (1950)
19) The Jane With The Green Eyes (1950)
20) Lola Brought Her Wreath (1950)
21) Lady, Toll The Bell (1950)
22) The Bride Wore Weeds (1950)
23) Don't Mourn Me Toots (1951)
24) This Dame Dies Soon (1951)

SERIES THREE
25) Baby, Don't Dare Squeal (1951)
26) Death Wore A Petticoat (1951)
27) Hotsy, You'll Be Chilled (1951)

28) It's Always Eve That Weeps (1951)
29) Frails Can Be So Tough (1951)
30) Milady Took The Rap (1951)
31) Women Hate Till Death (1951)
32) Broads, Don't Scare Easy (1951)
33) Skirts Bring Me Sorrow (1951)
34) Sadie Don't Cry Now (1952)
35) The Filly Wore A Rod (1952)
36) Kill Her If You Can (1952)

SERIES FOUR
37) Murder (1952)
38) Conflict (1952)
39) Tension (1952)
40) Whiplash (1952)
41) Accused (1952)
42) Killer (1952)
43) Suspense (1952)
44) Pursuit (1953)
45) Vengeance (1953)
46) Torment (1953)
47) Amok (1953)
48) Corruption (1953)

SERIES 5
49) Silken Menace (1953)
50) Nyloned Avenger (1953)

SPECIALS
Auctioned (1952)
Persian Pride (1952)
Desert Fury (1953)
One Man In His Time (1953)
Unseen Assassin (1953)
Deadly Mission (1953)

BROADS, DON'T SCARE EASY

HANK JANSON

First published in the united Kingdom in 2005 by
Telos Publishing Ltd
5A Church Road, Shortlands, Bromley, Kent, BR2 0HP
www.telos.co.uk

Telos Publishing Ltd values feedback. Please e-mail us with any comments
you may have about this book to: feedback@telos.co.uk

This edition © 2014 Telos Publishing Ltd

ISBN: 978-1-84583-876-8

Introduction © 2005 Steve Holland
Novel by Stephen D Frances
Cover by Reginald Heade
With thanks to Steve Holland
Cover design by David J Howe

The Hank Janson name, logo and silhouette device are registered
trademarks of Telos Publishing Ltd

First published in England by New Fiction Press, November 1951

British Library Cataloguing in Publication Data.
A catalogue record for this book is available from the British Library.

PUBLISHER'S NOTE

The appeal of the Hank Janson books to a modern readership lies not only in the quality of the storytelling, which is as powerfully compelling today as it was when they were first published, but also in the fascinating insight they afford into the attitudes, customs and morals of the 1940s and 1950s. We have therefore endeavoured to make *Broads, Don't Scare Easy*, and all our other Hank Janson reissues, as faithful to the original editions as possible. Unlike some other publishers, who when reissuing vintage fiction have been known edit it to remove aspects that might offend present-day sensibilities, we have left the original narrative absolutely intact.

The original editions of these classic Hank Janson titles made quite frequent use of phonetic 'Americanisms' such as 'kinda', 'gotta', 'wanna' and so on. Again, we have left these unchanged in the Telos Publishing Ltd reissues, to give readers as genuine as possible a taste of what it was like to read these books when they first came out, even though such devices have since become sorta out of fashion.

The only way in which we have amended the original text has been to correct obvious lapses in spelling, grammar and punctuation, and to remedy clear typesetting errors.

Lastly, we should mention that we have made every effort to trace and acquire relevant copyrights in the various elements that make up this book. However, if anyone has any further information that they could provide in this regard, we would be very grateful to receive it.

INTRODUCTION

From a cover that will have the 'eats, shoots and leaves' brigade scratching their collective heads, to the final sentence (does he die or is he sleeping?), *Broads, Don't Scare Easy* is a book full of questions. It holds the distinction of having one of the most sympathetic narrators in the whole Janson canon, a murderer who dreams of firing his gun and watching the bullet smash through meaty flesh. Early in the book, the narrator draws a bead on his fellow racketeer, Whitey, and imagines the bullet smashing through his face, 'his head jolting backwards, bone and blood spattering the car as lead tore out through the back of his skull. That made me feel really good.'

But Joey, the narrator, is unique. A one-off. Proof, if you needed more, that author Stephen D Frances often used the clichés of the gangster novel formula to produce something surprising and new. Frances had himself written enough formulaic gangster yarns to know what the clichés were, and dubbed Hank Janson the 'Best of Tough Gangster Authors' on dozens of covers. Was he consciously playing with the formula? Certainly. All the characters and every event in the plot of *Broads, Don't*

Scare Easy are carefully chosen specifically to create the situation that gives the book its climax. We can only speculate whether or not Frances deliberately chose to replace his usual coverline with a new one – 'Britain's Best-selling American Author' – eschewing the word 'gangster' deliberately for one of the rare occasions when gangsters and their molls actually did fill all the key roles in the book.

The phrase 'Best of Tough Gangster Authors' returned a couple of books later, perhaps to assure readers that this was the same Hank Janson of old, but was lost with the arrival of the fourth series, as the publishers tried to distance themselves from the problems then facing many of the gangster novel publishers over too-salacious covers. *Broads, Don't Scare Easy* was the third in a run of titles that the publisher New Fiction Press had chosen to modify to avoid problems with the police. The previous two, *Milady Took The Rap* and *Women Hate Till Death*, had both had their covers entirely replaced with plain-coloured wrappers with the Hank Janson silhouette. Rather than waste valuable cover stock, New Fiction Press's boss, Reg Carter, chose to use silver ink on the next two covers, entirely obliterating the girls featured in Reginald Heade's original artwork. The results were odd to say the least, and must have left the readers wondering what was happening.

The 'silvered' edition of *Broads* was published in November 1951. A second edition followed in December 1952, by which time the publishers were feeling confident enough to restore the original cover with a minor change to the price, which was 1/6 on the original Heade artwork but raised to 2/- when the book was first published.[1]

---

[1] The cover to this Telos edition of *Broads* has been reproduced from a

Broads was subsequently reprinted by Alexander Moring in 1958 under the shorter title *Don't Scare Easy*, with the text edited to remove hints of sadism. For instance, the scene in chapter seven at Madame Rozetti's cathouse was trimmed down. Where the original read ...

> Madame Rozetti chuckled, fluffed up her hair so her bejewelled fingers sparkled in the light. 'You know my girls. Which ones you wanting?'
> Maxie said quickly: 'Bright-eyes for me. Is she free?'
> Madame checked in a ledger she had on the reception desk. 'You're lucky, fella,' she chuckled. 'You know the way – Room 28.'
> Whitey had that mean twist to his lips. It gave him a sadistic satisfaction to know the girls hated him, tried every way they knew to avoid him. He went with the same way as he did everything, with his mean, twisted streak of cruelty well to the forefront.
> 'I'll take a gamble,' said Whitey. 'Run your finger down the list. Give me the first one you come to who's free.'

... the reprint trimmed this back to:

> Madame Rozetti chuckled and fluffed up her

cover proof of the original first edition, with the 1/6 price still intact, although it was only ever marketed at 2/-. The second book to feature a silvered cover, *Skirts Bring Me Sorrow*, has also been restored for the Telos edition, and also shows the original 1/6 price tag.

hair so her bejewelled fingers sparkled in the light. 'You know my girls,' she said.

Maxie said quickly: 'Bright-eyes for me.'

Madame checked in a ledger she had on the reception desk.

'You lucky, fella.'

Whitey had that mean twist to his lips. He knew the girls hated him, tied every way they knew to avoid him.

'I'll take a gamble,' said Whitey. 'Give me the first one you come to.'

To complete the reprint history of the book, *Don't Scare Easy* was reissued by Roberts & Vinter in 1961, although the actual book was simply the Alexander Moring edition with a new cover by Michel. When this did not use up the unsold stock, it was reissued again in around 1963 as part of the 'New Collectors series' with a cover by Noiquet. All told, we can guesstimate that the book sold something like 125,000 copies in its various editions, of which the edited Moring reprint is probably the most common.

I've mentioned before (in the introduction to *Accused*, for instance[2]) that excluding Hank Janson from the narrative allowed Steve Frances to write harder-edged stories: Hank's established character meant that he could never be immoral or weak in spite of his flaws; a novel without Janson was not so limited. In Joey, the narrator of *Broads*, Frances used this to full advantage.

Joey is introduced in the third-person prologue – the book switches to first person narration with Chapter

---

2 Telos Publishing, 2004

One – as part of a group of ragged, grimy kids fooling around in a vacant lot in an unnamed American city. The kids fall silent when Joey proudly shows them a gun. It glints where the sun catches it. Although they don't believe him when he claims that the gun is his, their startled awe is palpable, and Joey gets a momentary glimpse at the power and wonder they have for the weapon.

Guns were not widely available in Britain in 1951, but were still seen as a real threat. Unlike America, where the Second Amendment, ratified in 1791, enshrines the American citizen's right to keep and bear arms as part of the Constitution, the laws relating to gun control in Britain have changed over the years. The English Bill of Rights predated the Constitution. It was passed in 1689 in order to limit the powers of royalty following the dethroning of the Catholic King James, ending the concept of the divine right of kings and making them subject to the laws passed by Parliament. The new king and queen – William of Orange and his wife, Mary – agreed to the Bill during the coronation, and it was formally passed through Parliament and given the Royal Assent in December 1689. Within this act, citizens were given the right: 'that the subjects which are protestants, may have arms for their defence suitable to their conditions, and as allowed by law.' Where the Second Amendment was created in order to allow States to maintain a well regulated militia and, as part of the Constitution, has remained enshrined in law, the British Act made gun ownership subject to changing laws.

The major change in the law came with the Pistols Act 1903, which restricted the sale of revolvers, and the Firearms Act 1920, which meant that handguns and rifles had to be licensed by the police in order to prevent

The original edition, with its 'silvered over' cover.

'criminals or weak-minded persons and those who should not have firearms'[3] from obtaining weapons. Various additional laws and amendments were consolidated in the Firearms Act 1937. Increasing lawlessness in post-War Britain eventually led to the Prevention of Crime Act 1953, which made it illegal to carry in a public place any article 'made, adapted, or intended' for an offensive purpose; it also made carrying concealed weapons for defensive purposes illegal.

Written in 1951, *Broads, Don't Scare Easy* predated the Prevention of Crime Act, but was a reaction to the increasingly violent climate: there were two-and-a-half times as many crimes of violence in 1951 as in 1938, and three times the number of sexual crimes. Four police officers were murdered in 1951. The film *The Blue Lamp* (1950) included the shocking death of popular police constable Dixon, played by Jack Warner, who was shot twenty minutes into the movie by a young thug played by Dirk Bogarde.

Author Stephen Frances had his own attitude to

---

[3] To quote Home Secretary Edward Shortt.

guns, later saying, 'Unlike Mike Hammer and similar tough heroes, Hank Janson did not run around shooting and killing frequently and casually. A killing is a very serious matter, and Hank Janson treated it as a very serious action. This attitude reflects my own convictions.'

The Alexander Moring reissue

Without Janson as narrator, Frances was able to explore the power of the gun in an innovative and disturbing way. The skirmish that follows Joey's revelation of the gun leads to him being shot in the head.

When we next meet Joey, his injury (described later as 'like a big vee had been cleaved in my head. All around the place it was hairless, the white skin of my skull puckered and wrinkled, the cleavage so deep you could almost bury your fist in it.') has caused his mental growth to become stunted. He is slow on the uptake and has a child-like outlook but, as Joey insists:

> Maybe I was slow on account of that slug lodged in my brain. But being slow isn't being dumb. I might take longer to figure things out,

but I finally get there the same as anyone else.
Sometimes being slow at forming conclusions
is useful, stops a guy acting rashly.

Joey has obviously learned this little mantra from his friend Nick Fenner, who is Joey's best (and only) close friend. Being broader and taller than the other boys, he is known as Big Nick in the Prologue. Confident and strong, he's a natural leader and looks out for the weaker, highly-strung Joey.

Joey may be the narrator of the story but, ultimately, *Broads, Don't Scare Easy* is the story of Nick Fenner. It is Nick, as seen through Joey's eyes, who evolves over the course of the tale, where every other character desperately tries to maintain the status quo. Part of both the strength and the weakness of the novel is Frances's handling of the character. Nick Fenner conforms wholly to the gangster stereotype that was common in British gangster novels of the time. His introduction as a youngster instantly paints him as a potential criminal as he explains to Joey, 'One of these days I'm gonna have a gun like that. A repeater. My ole man says no guy's worth his salt unless he's gotta gun, same as the cops.'

When Joey is shot, Nick remains behind, leaning over Joey's convulsing body. 'He knelt over him for a long while, watching intently, obtaining from his vigil a strange sense of power and omnipotence,' and when the cops come, Nick slyly offers to name the shooter if he gets a reward. 'I suppose my name will get in the papers,' he says. 'They'll know me. Everyone will know me. I'll be famous.'

As the story proper takes off, we find that Nick has become a major racketeer, and his every action paints him blacker: he tries to frame a cop who will not turn a blind eye to crime and ends up shooting him; he has his sidekicks Maxie and Whitey beat up and drown a nosey reporter; and he rapes a drunk and unconscious young girl before dumping her naked on a park bench. Cathouse operator Madame Rozetti calls him 'the meanest, most selfish and hardest monster of a man I ever met or heard of,' and his every action backs up that claim.

At the same time, Nick is Joey's protector. The slow, dim-witted narrator adores Nick. Whitey and Maxie constantly insult his intelligence ('you big dope, you dumb-bell') and Lola, Nick's girlfriend, treats him as if he's sub-human. Nick jumps to Joey's defence, keeps Joey calm and offers him advice and friendship.

Eventually his friendship is repaid, as it is Joey who introduces Nick to Sheila, first introduced as a forlorn little runaway in threadbare clothes. With the help of Joey, she gets a job at Nick's nightclub, the *Devil's Dive*, and is discovered by Nick just as he is looking for a replacement for Lola. Frances sets up the situation so that we fully expect Nick to mistreat the girl horribly, and he does not.

This switch from sadistic rapist to a love-consumed repentant comes all too easily. It's a weakness in the novel. When he was writing *Broads*, Frances knew that his audience would be steeped in the kind of gangster fiction that he was trying to subvert; readers would expect Nick to be a monster, and that's what Frances gave them ... up to the point he turned the situation on its head. Reading the book in isolation fifty years on, the twist doesn't have the same shock value it would have had in 1951.[4] Instead,

---

[4] Nor does the mention of a flat having the luxury of a radio *and* a television set have the same impact it would have had in 1951, when there were only 764,000 licensed television sets in the UK.

Nick's sudden redemption and sacrifice seem somewhat contrived. Frances offers no explanation, and even Nick's protection of Joey doesn't hold up to examination. After all, Nick is willing to involve Joey in the double murder of 'Pop' Slack and his son, Jeff.

Yet redeemed he is. And the key to his redemption is Joey. The dummy. The prize dope. Poor Joey, whose simple naiveté disguises a murderous urge. The trauma of his shooting has left him with a deadly legacy:

> It was happening. I couldn't stop it. The hammering and the red flush expanding inside my brain. I was trembling all over, and now the sweat was coming, pouring out of me, soaking my clothes, so that when the fear hit me, it was like I was wet all over. I was scared it wasn't there, fumbled for it desperately, knowing they'd sneaked up on me and taken it, and knowing too that if I didn't find it, I'd die. I just had to find it. If I didn't find it, I'd die. Die! Die!

Desperately, Joey fumbles for the gun in his pocket. The touch of the smooth, comforting butt is only a partial relief. He needs to raise the gun, line up the sights on his tormentor. His hand trembles, but he draws a bead dead centre, right between the eyes. 'Can I shoot now, boss?' he asks Nick.

And Nick says yes. Yes, you can shoot him now.

Joey, the prize dope, suffers from obsessive-compulsive disorder. Not new to literature – Lady MacBeth's persistent hand-washing ('out, out damned spot') in Shakespeare's play dates back to the 17th Century – but scarce, and certainly a first in British gangster fiction. Nowadays, studies of OCD theorise that the problem lies in a dysfunction between the basal ganglia and frontal lobe of the brain, and treatment with Seratonin (one of the brain's main neurotransmitters) helps with these communication problems. In the early 1950s, OCD was thought to be a result of unconscious conflicts and mostly based on Freud's studies at the turn of the century; Freud concluded that the obsessive behaviour he saw in patients such as the famous 'Rat Man' was a result of 'Transformed self-reproaches which have re-emerged from repression and which always relate to some sexual act that was performed with pleasure in childhood.'

Frances identifies many of the traits of obsessive-compulsive disorder as we understand it today. It is nowadays classed as an anxiety disorder[5], triggered in Joey's case by taunts that cause him to panic; once he has entered this state, he must find the gun he constantly carries to assure himself that it hasn't been stolen. The final part of this compulsive ritual is to fire the gun at his persecutor.

For all his simplicity, Joey is actually one of the more complex characters in the novel. When he finds he has feelings for Sheila (although he does not understand them), he also finds that her voice ('like music') can bring on the same calmness that Nick's soothing can bring about. He doesn't understand the 'funny kinda feeling deep down inside' that he gets from seeing women. 'There was an urge inside me that wanted something. I was like a child crying for something and not knowing what it was.'

---

[5] At one time it was thought to be a kind of schizophrenia.

The sexual conflict is fuelled by Nick's insistence that, 'Dames are poison. They're all the same. You don't want no trouble with them ever.' A stripper at the club reinforces Nick's comments when she tells him, 'Dames are no good for you, Joey … You keep well away from them.'

If the reader expects Nick to remain true to the form he has shown earlier in the novel by mistreating Sheila, it's not a great step to imagine that the climax of the book would see Joey come to her aid. Frances manages to twist this all around in the final two chapters. Nick and Joey are going to be spending a long time together from now on. How that happens … well, you'll just have to read the book.

Steve Holland
Colchester, August 2004

PROLOGUE

The excited cries of the playing youngsters echoed across the vacant lot. Something had caught their attention, caused them to mill around in a tight little group, jostling, elbowing for position.

Suddenly an unusual silence came over them. A silence that was shocked and startled, so that if they'd noticed it, their parents would have come running across broken, rubble-strewn ground to lead their sons home before they were involved in trouble.

In the centre of the ring, one boy stood proudly showing something that glistened when the sun caught it.

The other boys looked at it in silence, a little afraid, very much awed.

'Where did you get it, Joey?' asked one at last.

Joey held it carefully. 'It's mine,' he said defiantly. 'I found it. It's mine!'

'G'wan! It's not yours. You didn't find it. It belongs to your Pop.'

Joey gave a hoist to his ragged, short trousers, wiped a grimy sleeve across his running nose. 'It's mine,' he protested furiously. 'I did find it, too! It's mine!'

The very force of his denial disproved his statement. The vehemence with which he contradicted the other boys proved their accusation.

'G'wan! It's your father's. Kids aren't allowed to have guns. You gotta have a licence to have a gun.'

'I gotta licence,' shouted Joey tearfully. 'It's my gun.'

Pride of possession had gripped him. The startled awe of the other boys gave him a momentary glimpse of power. He revelled in it and was reluctant to allow his moment of glory to slip through his fingers.

'It's loaded too,' he added fiercely. 'I'll show you. It's got real bullets.'

They didn't believe him, and gathered around as inexpertly he broke the gun at its breach, displayed the gleaming copper heads of live bullets.

'Your ole man'll lam the living daylights outta ya when he finds you've taken it,' said one boy, voice hushed with apprehension.

'It's mine!' shouted Joey fiercely. 'Bullets an' all!'

A smaller boy than the others, with mean little lips and a pale face that earned him the nickname of Whitey, sniffed contemptuously. 'Dat's nothin',' he sneered. 'My ole man's gotta better gat than that.'

They closed in around Joey, full of excited interest, vaguely aware they could taunt the highly-strung Joey unbearably if only they could find an opening.

A stocky, blue-eyed boy, with fair hair cropped close to his skull, saw the opening. 'I've got an idea,' he cried. 'We'll take the gun from him. Then his Pop will half-kill him.'

Quick to sense Joey's fear, the other boys moved in quickly, hustled Joey, who frantically thrust the gun away in his pocket, and began to strike out around him, desperate with tearful anger.

'It's my gun!' he sobbed fiercely as he hit out with hands and feet, almost crazy for fear the gun would be taken from him.

The fair boy, who had made the suggestion, doubled up in pain, hugging his belly where Joey's hard boot had landed. The boy's name was Jorgens, and he'd inherited a Swedish temper. 'Crucify the little devil!' he roared, with tears of pain running down his cheeks.

'It's my gun!' screamed Joey. 'Nobody's gonna take it! It's my gun!'

With their leader out of the fight, and Joey almost crazy with rage, the other boys fell back, just a little afraid of the violence of the emotions they'd aroused.

'He's gone crazy,' said one. 'He's scratching like a wildcat.'

'Crucify the little devil!' roared Jorgens.

They were boys of the same age, between ten and eleven – ragged, poorly clothed and ill-fed, typical children of the dead-ends. Children without a future, whose lives were already pointing along a downward path hedged with poverty, vice and corruption.

They had no sympathy for the crying, highly-strung boy who watched them fearfully, knowing that like ravenous wolves they would attack again in force, tearing at his mind and body.

One of the boys suddenly shouted, gleefully: 'I've got his gun! I've got his gun!' He flourished something that glistened in the sun, and the wolf-pack set up a derisive howl of triumph.

It was like a great wave of fear swamping over Joey, so immense and terrifying it shocked his mind. He saw the upraised belt, the flaming eyes of his father, and heard the thwack of leather before pain bit through him. He was frantic with terror, dived his hand into his pocket and almost cried with relief when his fingers closed around the butt of the revolver. Then he felt weak, drained of strength.

The other boys chortled. 'That scared him,' said one.

'Why don't you leave me alone?' pleaded Joey. 'Why don't you guys leave me alone?'

With the mercilessness of youngsters, they taunted him, gibed, laughed and insulted him until he was trembling half with rage and half with self-pity.

They were in the mood to continue their merciless derision until Joey finally broke and ran from them in tears. Then they would follow, still jeering, shouting insults and taunts.

But, as though by magic, the hoots of laughter suddenly died to silence. Another boy, not much older than the others but broader and taller, had arrived. He was quite young, but already his face showed he would be handsome. Already his black eyes reflected a fierce, merciless determination. He said quietly, but with such force of will-power the others obeyed him:

'Why don't you guys pipe down? Leave the kid alone, can't you?'

'We was only ribbing,' said Whitey.

The bigger boy regarded him solemnly. He was sure of himself, confident of his strength, and his name was Nicholas. The other boys called him Big Nick on account of his being broader and taller than any of them. He said quietly, without it seeming to be a challenge: 'Do you want I should tear your arm off and beat you to death with it?'

Whitey bit his lip, looked away from Nick, pretended he hadn't heard him.

'What's the matter, Joey?' asked Nick gently.

'They were gonna take my gun,' complained Joey. He took it from his pocket, displayed it. 'It's my gun,' he said. 'They wanted to take it.'

Nick glared around at the others. 'Why don't you fellas leave him alone?' he demanded. 'You're always ganging up on him.'

Whitey said, with an artful twist to his mean little lips: 'We was just fooling, Nick. Joey can't take it. He makes a squawk every time you rib him. We were gonna take his gun for a joke.'

Nick scowled darkly. 'Listen,' he said. 'If anyone's gonna take that gun, it's gonna be me. You shoulda asked me first.'

'It's my gun, Nick,' said Joey, desperately. 'You wouldn't wanna take it, would you? You wouldn't let them take it, would ya, Nick?'

The fear and anxiety of the smaller boy was flattery to Nick's swollen ego. 'Leave it to me,' he said, grandly. 'I'll kill anyone that takes it.'

As long as Nick was around, Joey knew he was safe. He tried to keep Nick by his side, showed him the gun, showed him the copper heads of the live cartridges. Nick was interested. He examined the gun with shining eyes. 'One of these days,' he told Joey, 'I'm gonna have a gun like that. A repeater. My ole man says no guy's worth his salt unless he's gotta gun, same as the cops.'

'This gun's mine,' said Joey, still persisting in the lie. 'It's loaded, too.'

'Sure it is,' said Nick. 'Sure it is. But don't let your ole man know you've taken it. He'll be real mad at you.'

The other boys drifted away. Someone produced a ball and a lump of old timber and they began playing a rude game of baseball.

Jorgens, who was still aching from the pain in his

groin, was watching Joey with narrowed eyes from a safe distance. He was waiting until Nick should leave him.

He didn't have to wait long for his opportunity. Nick's interest in the gun waned when he decided to show the other boys how to pitch to the batter. He left Joey, and immediately Jorgens, together with three of his friends, moved in on Joey.

They thrust at him, crowded around him, muffled his shrieks of alarm with their bodies. As he struck out frantically they grappled with him, held his arms, stamped heavy boots on his toes, while Jorgens surreptitiously plunged his hand into Joey's pocket, replacing the revolver with a heavy lump of metal.

They danced away from Joey, Jorgens brandishing the revolver, showing the world he'd got it. The other boys quickly crowded around Jorgens, all excitedly whooping.

It was several seconds before Joey realised the weight in his pocket was not the gun. When his fingers curled around the lump of iron, he was swept up anew by a wave of fear. He saw again the hard glint of his father's eyes, the upraised arm and the swinging strap. His mind shrank with terror from the swift pain that followed.

He found he was sweating with fear, his mind recoiling from the penalties incurred if his father should discover he'd taken the revolver. Fear allowed him just one angle of escape. He had to get that revolver back from Jorgens!

Unafraid now, cat-footed, Joey stalked determinedly towards his tormentor.

Sensing the sudden desperation and tenseness in the atmosphere, the other boys grew suddenly quiet, slipped back, leaving Joey and Jorgens facing each other.

One blond and taunting, the other desperately determined, spurred on by a great fear.

'Give it me!' mouthed Joey. His face worked with desperation, beads of perspiration standing out on his forehead.

Jorgens flourished the gun, grinned mockingly. 'Come and get it, sucker,' he sneered.

'I'll get it!' snarled Joey, and using the piece of iron as a menacing weapon, he advanced on Jorgens slowly.

There wasn't one boy who didn't sense the sudden difference in the atmosphere. This was no longer a childish prank. Here was a boy goaded beyond endurance, goaded so far the piece of iron in his hand had become a deadly weapon he would use without hesitation.

Jorgens, too, sensed the dangerous change in Joey. Fear leapt into his eyes as he stretched out one hand placatingly, backed a couple of paces. 'Just a minute, Joey,' he said. 'We was just playing. It was only fun.'

Joey said nothing. His eyes were blazing. He advanced on Jorgens steadily, hand upraised and anger written on every line of his face. 'Give it me!' he rasped.

He scared Jorgens. 'Get back, Joey,' he said. Instinctively, he raised the gun he held, pointed it at Joey. 'Get back, Joey!' he warned again. 'Get back or I'll shoot!'

Joey stopped, poised on the brink of indecision, arm upraised threateningly and anger smouldering in his eyes.

Nick, the one boy who had the leadership that could save the situation, stood on one side, calmly watching, one eyebrow upraised, as though he was speculating on the outcome.

Whitey suddenly added fuel to the fire. 'You

dope, Joey!' he yelled. 'He won't shoot. Joey, you sucker, go for him! Take the gun from him. You big dumb-bell! You big dope! Don't be afraid of him!'

The taunts struck home, caused the tight-lipped Joey to advance another pace.

Jorgens' face was white now. He was as desperately afraid as Joey had been a few moments earlier. 'I'll shoot, Joey,' he threatened. 'I'll kill you. I'll shoot.' The revolver was trained straight between Joey's eyes.

'Joey, you dope!' shrieked Whitey, jumping up and down excitedly. 'You big dumb-bell, you sap! Take it away from him! Sure you can get it. You can kill him now, you sap! Rush him!'

Even at that moment, Nick could have saved the situation, intervened between the two boys, silenced the one with words and the other with a gesture. But he hovered, watching with a strange, brooding glow in his eyes, almost as though he was hopefully anticipating the grim finale. As Joey trembled with rage, goaded almost beyond endurance, Whitey's voice sounded again: 'Sure you can, Joey. Sure you can kill him. Go for him, dope! Take the gun!'

Whitey's taunting words were all that were needed. They were like the pressing of an electric button. Joey exploded into movement, rushing towards Jorgens with arm upraised to smash, pound and pulverise. For a moment, Jorgens' feet were rooted to the ground with fear as he waited, undecided whether to drop the revolver and run or attempt to fight.

Joey swept down upon him, looming large and dangerous, the sun glittering on that upswinging, deadly piece of iron. An automatic self-defence mechanism was set off inside Jorgens. Almost without knowing it, his finger was pressing on the trigger, pulling harder and harder until, with a shattering impact, it seemed to explode in his ears and eyes as Joey was picked and hurled to one side by a giant, invisible hand.

For a moment, all of them were rooted to the spot while the crashing reverberation of that single shot echoed around them. Then they scattered, running blindly, pell-mell, stumbling, tripping, jumping across the broken masonry and loose bricks, scrambling frantically to get anywhere, somewhere out of reach of that awful thing that had happened.

Only one boy didn't run. Nick. With interested speculation in his eyes, he bent over Joey; watched the convulsive twitching of the small body. He knelt over him for a long while, watching intently, obtaining from his vigil a strange sense of power and omnipotence.

He was still kneeling there when folks who'd heard the shot began to arrive. Shirt-sleeved men, aproned women, men and uniformed cops, all white-faced and shocked.

'I suppose my name will get in the papers after this?' Nick asked the cop slyly.

The cop eyed him shrewdly. 'That ain't nothing to be proud about, son.'

'They'll know me,' said Nick proudly. 'Everyone will know me. I'll be famous.'

The cop snapped the band on his notebook, tucked it away in his tunic pocket.

'You'll learn, son,' he said heavily.

The ambulance was there now. They were lifting a small, blanketed figure on to a stretcher. The cop called to one of the stretcher-bearers. 'What d'ya think?'

The internee shook his head doubtfully. 'He's just gotta chance,' he said. 'Just a slender chance he'll pull through. But he'll never be the same.'

Nick asked the cop: 'Do I get a reward for telling the name of the guy that did it?'

1

Max pulled the car over to the side of the road, dropped speed until he was crawling at a walking pace. 'Is that the guy?' he asked, screwing up his eyes in an attempt to recognise the distant, uniformed figure further along the street.

Big Nick, who was sitting beside me on the back seat, leaned forward, peered over Whitey's shoulder. 'Can't see from here,' he said. 'Drive right past him.'

It amazed me how casual Nick's voice was. He's got a naturally deep, low-pitched voice, soft and musical. It's the kinda voice that makes you think of black velvet.

'It's not him,' growled Whitey in disgust, and there was nothing soft about his voice. It was like him, taut and jumpy.

Whitey wasn't the only one taut and jumpy. Me and Maxie as well were kinda toned up, over-excited. I always get that way when there's a job to do. Even a little job like this when there's practically no danger.

Yeah, this job was peanuts. A coupla fellas coulda taken care of it any time almost without thinking. It was that easy. It only became an interesting job on account Big Nick himself had taken a personal interest, wanted to see it handled proper.

We were right on top of the guy now; Maxie tooted his horn, and the cop who'd paused beneath a street lamp, looked up sharply, grinned as he recognised Whitey, and touched his peaked cap.

'Brake, Maxie,' ordered Nick lazily. 'I wanna talk to this guy.'

Maxie swerved into the kerb, slapped on the brakes. Whitey lowered his window, thrust his head out and looked back along the road. 'Hey, you!' he yelled.

The cop didn't exactly come running, but he walked a whole lot faster than cops usually walk on night duty.

'What's on your mind, Whitey?' he asked when he got level with us, panting slightly. Then for the first time be caught sight of Big Nick, touched his cap respectfully. 'Evening, Mr Fenner,' he said with careful politeness. 'I didn't recognise you at first. Is there something you want?'

Nick's broad shoulders bulked broadly as he spoke through the window, blocking my view so I couldn't see the cop. 'What time you off duty?' he asked.

There was a pause as the cop consulted his watch. 'In just ten minutes, Mr Fenner.'

'How're your folks?' asked Nick. His voice was like black velvet.

'Doing real fine, sir,' said the cop proudly. 'Thank you for asking.'

'Everything quiet? No trouble?'

'I'll say,' said the cop with satisfaction.

'Okay,' said Big Nick. He relaxed back in the seat. 'Drive on, Maxie,' he ordered.

Maxie let in the gear smoothly and the cop respectfully saluted again as our high-powered car effortlessly pulled away from the kerb like a silent ghost.

'Where to?' asked Maxie.

'Keep driving,' ordered Nick. 'We're in no hurry.'

Whitey half-turned to look over his shoulder at Nick. 'Ya don't havta worry yourself about this job, boss,' he drawled. 'Me and Maxie can handle it.'

'Yeah, we can .handle this, boss,' I interjected quickly. 'Me and Maxie can fix him fine.'

There was a sneer in Whitey's voice. 'Listen to him!' he jeered. 'The big dope!'

Big Nick said softly, smoothly: 'Cut it out, Whitey.'

I narrowed my eyes in the darkness and glared at Whitey. The guy was always riding me, always talking about me like I didn't know what time it was. Maybe I was slow on account of that slug lodged in my brain. But being slow isn't being dumb. I might take longer to figure things out, but I finally get there the same as anyone else. Sometimes being slow at forming conclusions is useful, stops a guy acting rashly.

'Let us drop you off at the apartment, boss,' said Maxie. 'Me and Whitey can handle it okay.'

'I can do it for you, boss,' I said eagerly. 'I don't need any help. I can do it alone.'

'Listen to him!' sneered Whitey. 'Just listen to him! The big dope!'

The bite in his voice stung deep. I kinda curled up inside, shrank up in my corner feeling mean and sulky. *That Whitey!* I told myself. One day I'd put a bullet through him. He deserved it. He talked like I hadn't got no brains at all.

'Cut it out, Whitey,' rapped Big Nick again, and now the black velvet sounded hard and brittle.

Having him take my side like that made me feel good again, kinda warmed inside. Big Nick always made me feel good. He was my friend!

Sure, he was my boss. But he was my friend, too; always slapping down the guys who got smart with me. He'd always been that way as far back as I can remember, right back to the time I came out of hospital after the quacks had admitted defeat, said the bullet was lodged beneath delicate brain tissue and they daren't operate.

'Aw, jeepers!' protested Whitey. 'Can't a guy have a little fun and ...'

'Cut it out!' rasped Nick, and his voice was like a whiplash. Then, as Whitey lapsed into silence, he added softly: 'How many more times am I gonna warn you guys not to get him excited?'

I didn't wanna cause Nick trouble. I knew how he worried about me, and I didn't want him to worry. He was my pal, looked after me. I didn't want him worried on my account.

'I'm not getting excited, boss,' I told him.

'Shuddup, Joey,' he growled. 'Just sit quiet and shuddup.'

He didn't mean anything when he talked to me that way. He talked to most everyone that way. It was a kinda habit.

'You want I should drive around the park a coupla times?' asked Maxie.

'I want you should drive,' said Nick. 'I don't care where.'

It was a quiet night and dark. There was no noise except the hum of the engine and the soft swish of the tyres. I settled back in the seat, closed my eyes and felt warm and happy inside. Having Big Nick as a pal made me a lucky guy. There wasn't anyone to touch Nick. He was the best guy on earth. He always gave me this warm, happy feeling inside. Gee, I guess I almost loved that guy.

Suddenly I couldn't feel the weight of it in my pocket and it scared me. I was so scared that for seconds I was paralysed with the shock of it. I felt the strength drain out of me and my hands began to tremble. They'd taken it away from me! They were all scheming to kill me and they'd stolen it from me. They were closing in now – ugly, monstrous, leering, jeering faces. The sweat sprang out all over my skin, ice-cold and soaking my underclothing. They were holding me down, great weights holding me down, iron bands around my wrists and my ankles so my body vibrated like a tuning-fork as I strained to escape. I strained, sweated, felt my muscles bulging, heard my bones creak and knew I'd go crazy if I couldn't snap the fetters.

They snapped!

Frantically I plunged my hand in my pocket, knowing if it wasn't there I'd die of it. Then great relief swept over me, I relaxed, cried with thankfulness as my fingers closed around the butt of the gun, felt its comforting weight.

'He's off again,' said Whitey.

'Leave him alone,' Big Nick said in his casual kinda way.

Maxie chuckled. 'Let 'em have it, Joey,' he encouraged. 'Give it 'em, fella.'

That's what I'd been waiting to hear. My hand trembled with excitement as I brought the gun from my pocket.

Maxie was watching me through the driving mirror. 'Take it easy, Joey,' he said. 'Take it slow and easy.'

I concentrated, tried to hang on to that thought. *Take it slow and easy. Take it slow and easy.*

It helped. My hand was only trembling a little now.

I raised it, squinted through the sights, trained them on Whitey and drew a bead dead centre of his forehead.

'Watch out, fellas,' warned Maxie. 'He's dangerous. He's gotta gun.' There was a chuckle in his voice.

Whitey stared at me evilly, his black eyes glinting with amusement. I could have pin-pricked the place where the lead would smash into his forehead.

'Ain't he the boy, now?' said Maxie.

'Look at the dope!' jeered Whitey. 'Look at his hand trembling.'

'You've gotta do better than that, kid,' said Maxie. 'You've gotta keep your hand firm. Rigid, like a bar of steel.'

I tried hard. The sweat was oozing out of me again.

'That's better,' soothed Maxie. 'You're as steady as a rock.'

'The poor dope!' sneered Whitey.

Jeepers, how I hated that guy! Always acting like I was dumb or something. The hatred flooded my mind so I could think of nothing else. 'Can I kill him now?' I asked.

'Sure,' said Maxie. 'You can kill him.'

I wasn't asking Maxie. I was asking Nick. When he didn't reply, I repeated the question. 'Can I kill him now, boss?'

'I warned you fellas not to get him excited,' growled Nick.

I wondered which of us he was talking to, because he was looking out the window. I waited and he didn't take notice of me. I held the gun even more firmly, licked my lips. 'Can I kill him now, boss?' I pleaded.

He sighed wearily. 'Okay,' he said. 'You can kill him.'

My heart beat with exultation. I glared through the

sights, concentrated on that point midway between Whitey's eyes and jerked my finger against the trigger.

As the hammer clicked on the empty cartridge, I saw just the way it should be, his head jolting backwards, bone and blood spattering the car as lead tore out through the back of his skull. That made me feel really good. I chuckled deep down in my chest, and the way Whitey's black eyes glittered at me made it even funnier.

'Okay, Joey,' snapped Maxie. 'That's enough. Put it away now. You're safe now. Nobody's gonna take it away from you.'

It was good to know I could keep it. I slipped it back into my pocket, held it against my side, so I could still feel it and know nobody was stealing it when I wasn't looking.

'I warned you fellas,' gritted Big Nick. 'Don't be too smart. Cut that stuff out when I tell you.'

Whitey muttered something below his breath, turned around and stared out through the windscreen.

Big Nick told me gently: 'You're okay now, Joey. We're all pals. You're one of us. Understand, Joey? You're as good as any of us, maybe a little better. And you're smart, too, smart as paint. Understand ? '

Gee, how I loved that guy! He could make me feel so good just talking that way. He told the truth, too. Sure, I was as smart as paint. I was as good as any of them. I was as strong as a lion and as smart as Einstein. A warm, happy glow suffused me. 'I feel good,' I said.

'Sure you feel good,' said Big Nick. 'You got a little sweaty a way back. But you're okay now.'

I thought about it. Yeah, he was right. I had been a little sweaty, kinda hazy. Maybe I shouldn't have pulled my gun on Whitey that way. But they made me do it. But it was all so dreamlike, I wasn't even sure I'd pulled that gun.

'Don't you think about it anymore, Joey,' said Big Nick.

That was good advice, too. I closed my mind, wouldn't allow myself to think about the gun.

'We've been driving around half an hour,' announced Maxie.

'All right, then,' said Big Nick. 'Turn around. Drive back and keep circling around that block until we see him.'

As Max swept the car around in a smooth, silent arc, I felt once more the tensed-up feeling I get just before I'm gonna do a job. I kept telling myself this job was different, it wasn't dangerous. But, just the same, I couldn't prevent myself feeling tense and strung-up.

We were gonna give a guy the works. He was a no-account guy, a cop named Bannister. But cops are different from other guys. Other guys you can stand in a pail of cement until it sets, then drop them off a bridge so they stand on the river bed until nothing's left of them to stand.

But cops are different!

Ordinary guys can have an accident, get run down by a car, impale themselves on a knife, have a shooting accident or fall from a tall building.

But cops never do these things. Not unless it's a *real* accident.

It was on account of cops being so special that Big Nick wanted to be around to make sure this job was done just the way he wanted.

I didn't feel sorry for Bannister. He was a dope. Any guy's a dope who tries to swim upstream when he can float with the tide.

Bannister was a new cop, just drafted over from Washington. Just an ordinary, twenty-dollar a week flatfoot wearing a uniform the same as a hundred thousand other cops. Yet the dope had to act like he was something special.

Big Nick had been reasonable. Nick's always reasonable. He's so reasonable, the Police Commissioner's got a safe job, the cop Captain owns one of the swellest joints on South Side, and there's not a cop on the force who doesn't double his wages.

They're entitled to. The one-armed bandits, the crap games, pool-rooms, numbers, gaming tables and cat houses pay off well. There's good pickings for everyone, the cops too, which makes everyone happy.

Because the public are happy. Sure they're happy. There isn't a workman who doesn't like his flutter on the gees, there's not a working dame who's not prepared to spend a coupla dimes for the chance of winning enough dough in the numbers racket to buy herself a mink coat. Cat houses are clean, a guarantee of health for guys who might otherwise pick up a tramp on the streets and get sicker than with Yellow Jack. One-armed bandits can be useful to a guy who's waiting for his dame on the corner and bungs an idle nickel in the machine that wins a pocketful sufficient to cover his expenses for the evening.

The way I see it, I figure Big Nick earned the esteem of the public for organising things in his district so the public could go on having fun.

Not everyone could have organised it the way Big Nick did. Cat houses, the numbers rackets, one-armed bandits and the rest of those things are against the law. It needed a clever guy to arrange everything so the public could get what it wanted.

Big Nick fixed it the right way and the best way. Sure, there's money in running the numbers racket. You don't expect anyone to work for nothing, least of all Big Nick. But the dough kicked in by the public, he split many times. The Police Commissioner lived like an English lord with a butler, a chauffeur and a big, stone house built to look like a castle.

He was entitled to. He lived that way on account he used his head, allowed the public to have the things they wanted, instead of cracking down on them, sending out his cops to stop them having fun.

Nick had a nice set-up, and everyone was happy. The public were happy, Big Nick was happy and the cops were happy. There was just one thing wrong with the set-up. Bannister!

How can a cop be so dumb?

The first day Bannister was registered on the force, the cop Captain treated him right, slipped a twenty-dollar bill into his hand.

Bannister stared at it, looked up at the cop Captain suspiciously. 'What's this for?' he demanded.

'That's for being smart,' said the cop Captain. 'Nobody on the force has the pull over anyone else. We level right the way along the line. Everyone plays ball and it pays off equally all round.'

Bannister looked puzzled but pocketed the dough. An hour later, he came in off his beat with Legs Simon in tow. Legs Simon was hopping mad on account Bannister had busted up one of the richest poker schools he'd organised in the past six months. Legs indignantly demanded to see the cop Captain, his mouthpiece, Big Nick and the President of the United States all at the same time.

The cop Captain seated Legs in his office to cool off with a box of cigars and a bottle of whisky for company. Meantime he took Bannister to a quiet room where he could draw him a picture.

But Bannister didn't see reason. Bannister claimed he was a cop and was doing his duty. He insisted on pressing the charge, wrote it in the charge book himself, and Big Nick had to put up a twenty grand bond for Legs Simon. Furthermore, to make the records look good, the following morning the Judge had to fine Legs Simon ten grand.

That hurt Big Nick. It cost him dough, and losing dough always hurt Nick. As organiser, Big Nick had to accept the final responsibility. He was liable for Legs Simon's fine, and what with the cops getting such a big cut on his earnings, Nick had to dig deep down in his bankroll.

You'd have thought that having shown his independence, Bannister would have learnt sense. But the guy was just dumb. The next night, he brought in Spike Mullins, who's a collecting agent for the numbers rackets.

The night after that, Mother O'Riley and twenty of her girls were being lined up before the bench.

The greatest danger to a precision made, well-oiled and smoothly working machine is one tiny, insignificant grain of sand!

In three days, a tiny grain of sand disrupted our machine so murderously it nearly seized up. Nick told the Commissioner bluntly there would be no more splits for him until Bannister ceased interfering with the organisation.

That sure caused consternation. All the cops from the Commissioner down to the most humble flatfoot were as dependent upon their split as upon their wages.

The answer should have been easy for the Commissioner. Fire Bannister.

But it wasn't so easy. The cop Captain had turned up Bannister's records, discovered he'd passed his police tests with flying colours, earned good merit certificates and was recommended for early promotion.

That wasn't a serious obstacle. Even the best of cops can take a tumble. But Bannister had connections! His father was a cop Captain in Washington, and he had an uncle in the Feds.

Bannister had confidently given the cop Captain a broad hint he wasn't gonna be sacked easily. If he was, Washington and the Feds would be wanting to know the ins and outs of the dismissal.

It was victory for Bannister. The cop Captain daren't sack Bannister without good reason, while, single-handed, Bannister was disrupting a beautiful, easily-running set-up that suited everyone else.

It was Nick who came up with the answer. He was always smarter than anyone else. So smart he didn't even tell the Commissioner about it.

'You get rid of that guy,' he told him. 'I don't care how you do it – just get rid of him!'

'But,' protested the Commissioner helplessly, 'what can I do? I'm powerless.'

'You get your cut for keeping things sweet,' said Nick. 'So just keep 'em sweet.'

It wasn't until we'd left the Commissioner's office that Nick told us what was at the back of his mind.

'There's only one way to get rid of Bannister,' he gritted. 'He's got to be discredited. He's gotta be thrown off the force in disgrace, and there has to be a damned good reason for sacking him.'

'What d'you think I should do?' demanded Whitey. 'Hypnotise him and tell him to rob a bank?'

'Hypnotising him won't be necessary,' said Nick

smoothly. 'And robbing a bank's too big a project.' He kinda hummed a little tune to himself. Then he added thoughtfully: 'I think a little petty robbery is more in Bannister's line. It won't be a big enough scandal to get publicity. But it'll be enough to earn him a stretch.'

Sure, Nick was smart. He had an answer for everything. He liked things done right, too. That's why he was with us tonight. And that's why we were driving the silent streets in the middle of the night on the watch for that dope Bannister now pounding his beat.

Yeah, Bannister had it coming to him. Tonight he was gonna be discredited.

2

'That must be him,' said Maxie.

'There's two of them,' said Whitey, peering through the windscreen, screwing up his eyes.

'Drive past slowly,' ordered Nick. 'We can always turn around.'

We drove past at a walking pace, and Whitey grunted with satisfaction. 'That's him!'

'How d'ya like that?' demanded Maxie. 'He takes anything – the small fish as well as the big!'

'She's only a kid,' said Whitey. 'Shows the kinda cop he is. Won't even give a kid a break.'

'Pull up here and wait for him,' instructed Nick.

Maxie nailed the car, switched off the engine. Nick was as calm as though he was sipping tea in the Ritz. He took out his gold cigarette case, calmly lit up. Whitey was nervous and jumpy. He kinda squared his shoulders when he opened his mackintosh, so he'd be able to get at the revolver in his shoulder holster without difficulty.

Maxie was watching Bannister in his driving mirror. 'He's almost on top of us,' he warned.

'Let's go,' said Nick. He leaned forward to open the car door. 'Let's do it right, huh?' he said. 'Quiet and easy, no trouble. Understand?'

We piled out of the car as Bannister got level with us. The dame he had by the arm was a nondescript, mousy little thing, shabbily dressed and with big brown eyes that were badly scared. She couldn't have been more than nineteen.

Big Nick lazily straddled himself across the sidewalk, tossed away his half-smoked cigarette, took his cigarette case from his pocket and lit up another. The way he stood there completely blocked Bannister's path.

Bannister wasn't totally dumb. He knew it meant trouble and watched with narrowed eyes as Whitey and Max lined themselves up on either side of Nick.

Bannister's fingers clutched more tightly around the young dame's arm so she gave a little whimper of pain. 'Clear the way there, let me through,' growled Bannister.

Maybe he figured he had corner street boys to deal with who'd be scared by a harsh voice. If so, he'd got Nick sized up wrongly. Nick didn't scare easy. In fact, Nick didn't scare at all – ever!

It was almost elegant the way Nick sucked leisurely at his cigarette, lazily blew a thin plume of smoke upwards and over the cop's head. Nick could do that kinda thing well, carry it off easily. He had a gentlemanly way, looked like a gentleman, too, with his broad-brimmed, black felt fedora and smart black overcoat. In fact, Big Nick had everything; tall, broad shoulders and a handsome face with eyes that were large and hypnotic.

'What's the trouble?' asked Nick pleasantly.

'What's it to you?' growled Bannister. 'Outta my way!'

Nick smiled softly, blew more smoke impudently

into Bannister's face. 'What's the little dame done?'

Bannister took a deep breath, seemed to swell up like a turkey cock. He was a young cop, broad and strong. You could see right away he had ideas about promotion, wanted to get to the top and stay there and wasn't too particular how he did it. 'I'll give you guys just three seconds to get outta my path,' said Bannister, and his hand made half a movement towards the Police Special .38 in his hip pocket.

It was almost lazy the way Big Nick took a step forward. He was so close to Bannister their chests were almost touching. At the same time, Maxie, Whitey and me moved in as well, kinda surrounded Bannister.

Whitey did it so skilfully I didn't even see his gun. Bannister's jaw tightened and a frosty look came into his eyes as he felt the steel muzzle gouging hard into his side.

'You didn't oughta treat a young dame that way,' said Big Nick reproachfully. The little dame looked at him with wide, terrified eyes. Her lip trembled like she was on the point of crying, and she gave a little whimper of pain as Bannister gouged his fingers even more deeply into her arm.

I'll hand it to Bannister. He had guts. There was no trace of fear in his voice. 'You guys are asking for trouble,' he warned. 'Real trouble. This is gonna get you in deep with the Feds.'

The little dame musta been in a haze. None of the conversation made sense to her. It would have done, if she'd seen the gun Whitey was holding.

'You don't wanna pinch the dame,' drawled Nick. 'Let her go.'

The cop's hand was fastened around her arm like bands of steel. 'You guys have still got a chance,' he warned. 'Get going before I change my mind.'

I had to admire the guy, because either he had guts or was too dumb to figure what a spot he was in.

Big Nick chuckled. Lazily he took his cigarette from his mouth and, just as lazily it seemed, stubbed the glowing end into Bannister's hand, the hand holding the dame.

A startled gasp of pain whistled through Bannister's teeth as he snatched back his hand. In the same moment, his other hand began to come into action, drew back to lash out at Big Nick. But Whitey was right there, grabbing the cop's clenched fist, stabbing his gun barrel hard into his side so that he wheezed with agony.

'Get the dame outta here, Joey,' ordered Nick swiftly. 'We'll take care of him.'

She was scared as hell, open-mouthed, not understanding what was happening. I grabbed her arm, propelled her rapidly along the street towards the intersection. 'Hurry along, kid,' I growled. 'You don't wanna spend the night in the can, do you?'

She didn't. She scurried along beside me, throwing anxious glances over her shoulder as though afraid Bannister might set off after her again. She didn't need to worry. It didn't look like that was gonna happen. I couldn't see much of Bannister, because the other three had crowded around him. It looked like he was awful busy.

I stopped to get my breath as soon as we were around the corner. She was breathing hard, too. I couldn't be sure if it was from nervousness or from hurrying.

'It's okay now, kid,' I said, breathing heavily. 'You scram.'

'You mean …' she faltered.

'Sure,' I said. 'You won't have any more trouble with that lug. Just beat it.'

She stood staring at me, forlorn, frail and very young. She aroused in me a kinda fatherly sympathy. I wondered why a dame so young and so pathetic should be out so late. 'What did he have on you, anyway?' I demanded.

'He – he was arresting me for – vagrancy! 'Her voice tailed off. She wasn't very far from tears.

'Get it off your chest, kid,' I advised. 'Tell me. You won't die of shame.'

It all came out in a rush. 'I've got nowhere to go,' she half-sobbed. 'I've got no money. I was just walking along the road and–'

Life can be tough at times. I thrust my hand in my pocket, pulled out a five-dollar bill. 'Here, take this,' I growled. 'Buy yourself a night's sleep. Feed up some place tomorrow.'

She looked at the money through a mist of tears. She just couldn't believe anything so wonderful was happening.

'Tuck it away, kid,' I said gruffly. 'And remember to keep out of sight of strong-arm cops.'.'

'You're so kind,' she quavered. 'You and that other gentleman, the man who made him let me go. You're so kind.' Her voice kinda broke.

'G'wan. Beat it now,' I growled. 'Don't hang around.'

She looked up at me and her eyes were shining and filled with tears. She had a pinched little face, mousy-coloured hair that straggled from beneath a dusty old felt hat. The coat she wore was drab and threadbare. Yet the happiness and gratefulness in her shining eyes seemed to transform her so although she was nothing but a drab, mousy-looking dame, she seemed to radiate happiness.

'Gee. You've been good, mister!'

'Okay, now beat it.'

'That other man, too.. The handsome one.'

She meant Big Nick. 'Okay,' I growled. 'Now beat it, will ya?'

'You did it for me,' she said wistfully. 'It ain't gonna cause no trouble, is it?'

'It might if you don't beat it. G'wan now. Scram, will ya?' I gave her a light push, made shooing motions with my hands. 'For crying out loud,' I rasped. 'Get going, will ya?'

She stumbled away from me reluctantly, looked over her shoulder, kinda hesitated. 'G'wan,' I yelled. 'Get cracking. He's coming after you. Beat it, will ya, ya dope!'

She sure was scared of going to gaol. Her worn shoes beat a rapid tattoo on the pavement. I watched until she was out of sight, merging into the shadows beyond the far street lamps, and even the clip-clop of her heels was swallowed up in the darkness.

I walked back around the corner to the deserted sidewalk. The car was drawn up into the kerb, waiting for me.

'What the hell kept ya?' demanded Big Nick as I came up. He was sitting in the front now next to Maxie. Bannister was sitting in the back, glowering, with Whitey sitting smack up against him like a long-lost brother. I squeezed in back, the other side of Bannister.

'Okay, Max,' ordered Nick. 'Don't kill time anymore.'

Whitey chuckled as Max pulled out from the kerb.

He's a guy with a twisted sense of humour, always trying to scare other folks. 'What else are we gonna kill, boss?' he asked with an evil glitter in his eyes. He was looking steadily at Bannister.

'Cut that out!' rasped Nick.

If Whitey was trying to throw a scare into Bannister, he didn't succeed. The cop just breathed hard, clenched his fists tightly on his knees.

'I was kidding,' defended Whitey.

We all knew he was kidding. Except maybe Bannister. Killings are serious matters at any time, any place. Killing was commonplace during prohibition, when inter-state police action wasn't synchronised. There were too many beer barons in the business those days. Competition was high, and some of it had to be eliminated. The boys used machine guns and bombs to help along the elimination.

But that was a quarter of a century ago. Things are different now. The rackets are run differently now – well organised, and the wheels greased with greenbacks, so there isn't anyone who doesn't get his pay-off. The rough-and-tumble stuff is over, and gang wars are finished. The guys at the top today are gentlemen. Like Big Nick. They belong to the best clubs, know the best folks, dine with senators and play golf at weekends.

Naturally, as with any other business, things don't run smoothly all the time. Occasionally, very occasionally, a little difficulty crops up and has to be handled. But it isn't the same as gang war, the retaliation killings and muscling-in on someone else's territory with strong-arm men. Nowadays it's the tactful disposal of an embarrassing factor. It always happens clean, too. Usually a car accident or falling off a high building.

Yeah, killing a guy is sometimes a necessity. But it

has to undertaken with extreme caution.

Killing a cop is out of the question.

A cop-killing brings down the Feds quicker than an inter-state bank robbery. It's hell then. The local cop force is overhauled, the city's turned inside out and the Police Commissioner stands by hopelessly, knowing the attention of Washington is focused on him.

Yeah, cop-killing is something to steer away from. That's why Big Nick was along tonight, to make sure everything went off smoothly. He'd known Whitey was joking, but just the same, he growled: 'Cut out that kinda talk, Whitey. I don't wanna hear it. Not even in joke.'

'Jeepers, creepers!' mumbled Whitey.

'Aw, let the cop sweat,' growled Maxie.

Bannister kinda squared his shoulders. I could sense arrogance and confidence flooding outta him. He said in an ugly voice: 'You rats can't scare me. You're gonna find yourselves in real trouble for this – real trouble!'

3

Everything was planned with the efficiency Big Nick displayed with everything he did.

Tobias Slack and his son Jeffrey were gonna be the principal witnesses against Bannister. Nick had chosen them with care, partly because of their jeweller's shop, partly because they lived on the premises, and partly because they'd never had trouble of any kind with the police previously.

There was another reason, too. A reason which wasn't known to many people. Tobias Slack was the cashier for the numbers racket in the district. Like everyone else, Tobias was going to feel the pinch if Bannister succeeded in summoning the numbers agents and listing heavy fines against them.

Jeffrey Slack cautiously opened the shuttered shop door, and we urged Bannister inside. Whitey directed him to take a chair in the centre of the shop, stood behind him pressing the gun into his ribs.

Nick stood in the centre of the shop, tall, broad and imposing, like he had a spotlight on him. He lit another cigarette, glanced around slowly as he did so.

The shop shutters were down, bolted firmly in

position. Only a few rays of light escaped into the darkness through the ventilator high up in the shutters. Nick grunted with satisfaction as he saw the doors of the glass showcases broken open, the display trays pulled out, emptied of their contents and scattered on the floor. He looked at Tobias Slack and his son, both clad in their pyjamas as Nick had instructed, and asked softly: 'How did he get in?'

Tobias's eyes gleamed. 'Musta used a jemmy,' he chuckled.

'Hear that, Maxie?' drawled Nick. 'He musta used a jemmy on the door.'

Max grinned, dived down in his pocket and drew out the jemmy he'd brought along with him. We watched as he went out through the shop door, closed it behind him. There was a furrow of perplexity on Bannister's brow. He didn't get any of this. He licked his lips, glared around. 'What are you guys playing at?' he demanded.

'Quit squawking!' rasped Whitey. He gouged the gun-muzzle into Bannister's side, using unnecessary force. Bannister's teeth clicked shut like a trap and his knuckles gleamed whitely. That jab had hurt. You could tell from the way he screwed up his eyes. But it did more than hurt. It goaded him to explosion point. You can goad anyone, even a mild guy, to the point where they blow their top. And Bannister wasn't mild!

Nick was watching Bannister. He saw the danger signal. 'Better take it easy, copper,' he warned. 'Getting tough won't do you any good.'

Maxie was working on the door now. I could hear the soft scraping as he inserted the keen blade of the finely-tempered steel in the crack of the door jamb. He began levering, and it was like the tiny scratching of mice. Even when the hinges gave and the door splintered inwards, it didn't make all that much noise.

Maxie forced his way inside through the gap between the door and the doorpost and grinned broadly.

'You're not the only one who stops up nights,' snarled Big Nick. 'Bolt that door back in position before someone gets curious.'

Bannister still didn't get it. His forehead puckered as he watched Maxie carefully prop the forced door back into its frame. There was a kinda tenseness about him, a kinda rolled-up spring tenseness, so we knew he'd erupt into action the first chance he got.

Maxie grinned with satisfaction, wiped his handkerchief across his sweating forehead.

'The jemmy!' snapped Nick irritably. 'Whad'ya waiting for?'

Maxie used his handkerchief to wipe the jemmy clean of fingerprints. Then he crossed to Bannister, still holding one end of the jemmy in the handkerchief.

'Catch hold of that!' rasped Whitey in the cop's ear. Bannister glared around at him. Then slowly he turned his head back to face Maxie.

'Grab that jemmy!' gritted Whitey.

Reluctantly, Bannister reached for it, gingerly touched one end.

'Get a good grip on it!' rasped Whitey. 'Grip it good and hard. Try to twist it outta his hand.'

Whitey punctuated his sentences with savage jabs from the gun. It musta been wearing to Bannister. That gun-muzzle was painful. There was sweat on his forehead as his fingers tightened around the jemmy, clenched it tightly, tried to twist it from Maxie's grasp.

'Okay,' snapped Whitey. 'That's enough.' Then, as Bannister released the jemmy, relaxed back in his chair, Maxie tossed the jemmy towards the door. It fell on the floor, mute evidence to a crime.

It wasn't until then that Bannister realised what was gonna happen. I saw the incredulity in his eyes, the thunderstruck expression on his face. But Nick was already rushing on, arranging every detail.

'You,' he said, pointing at Jeffrey Slack. 'Let's have a look at you.'

Jeffrey was a young fella, tall and gangly, with a hank of black hair that hung down over one eye, and a loose jaw. He shuffled forward sheepishly, stood still while Nick looked him over.

'What happened?' asked Nick.

Jeffrey shuffled his feet in embarrassment, ran his fingers through his hair and stammered: 'I heard a noise, see. In the shop. So I woke Pop and we both came down together. There was this guy here filling his pockets with rings and stuff he'd taken from the trays.' He thumbed towards Bannister.

'You're sure this is the guy?' asked Nick.

'Sure I'm sure,' said Jeffrey with stolid conviction. 'As soon as I saw him, he rushed me with the jemmy.' He nodded towards the jemmy lying on the floor at the door.

'Then what happened?'

'He tried to brain me,' said Jeffrey indignantly. 'But I managed to grab his arm, grappled with him. We rolled all over the place, all the time him trying to bash my head in. Then Pop arrived.'

Nick turned to Maxie. 'The kid said he was stuffing his pockets with rings and jewellery.'

Maxie grinned, picked up a handful of assorted jewellery from an up-ended tray and scattered it across the floor. He took another handful, walked across to Bannister, dropped it into the pocket of his tunic.

The cop still couldn't believe it was happening. It

stunned him that he should be framed in such a cold-blooded fashion. He swallowed hard, and his thick neck was red right up to the ears. It looked to me like Whitey was gonna have to watch him. Pretty soon that cop would be good and mad.

'For a guy that's had a life and death struggle, you look mighty serene,' Nick told Jeffrey.

'I suppose so,' said Jeffrey ruefully. He raised his fingers to his hair, fluffed it over his head. Then he shredded the buttons from his pyjama jacket, tore one of the sleeves. 'How's that?' he asked brightly, like he'd done something clever.

'Not enough,' said Nick curtly. He looked at Maxie again. 'Fix him up, fella.'

'Sure,' said Maxie. 'I'll fix him.' He walked across to Jeffrey, who stood waiting patiently. The kid never knew it was coming. Maxie's fist caught him flush in the eye, sent him hurtling backwards, shoulders thudding against the ground. He was three-quarters dazed when Maxie grabbed him by the collar, dragged him around the floor, rumpling the pyjamas and covering them with dust. That sock in the eye musta hurt. Already it was swelling and reddening. In no time it would be turning a deep purple.

The kid began to squawk. Anyone would. It wasn't pleasant being dragged around that way.

'Okay, Maxie,' drawled Nick. 'That's enough, finish him off now.'

Maxie stood back, allowed the kid to climb to his feet. The kid was whimpering now, hot tears of pain scalding his good eye and his shoulder bleeding where a nail in the rough flooring had ripped the skin.

Once again the kid didn't know it was happening. He'd reached his feet when Maxie's knuckles lashed with the speed of a striking snake. It was a carefully chosen blow, landed flush on the kid's nose, pulping flesh and bone. The kid sat down hard, blood spurting from his nose like a fountain.

Nick eyed Jeff with satisfaction as he sat on the floor, both hands clasped to his face, blood trickling through his fingers, dripping on his bare chest and staining his torn pyjamas.

'That's fine,' he said. 'That's real fine. The kid sure did put up a fight.' Leisurely he turned to stare at Bannister. 'You didn't come out of that too well either,' he grinned evilly.

Bannister eyed Max warily as he advanced on him. He clenched his teeth, breathed hard as Max ripped buttons from his tunic, tore his collar.

'Okay, copper,' snarled Whitey. 'Down on your knees.'

The cop was really beginning to realise what he was up against. He was unwilling and apprehensive. But, as Whitey once again jabbed the gun-muzzle into the same inflamed side, he winced, went down on his knees in front of his chair.

'Bend over,' gritted Whitey. 'Bend right down, forehead touching the floor.'

No-one's ever tried to pretend Maxie is a gentleman. He didn't act like a gentleman either. Because no gentleman ever uses his feet as Maxie did.

His heavy boot caught Bannister flush in the centre of his puss as he lowered his head. The vicious kick snapped his head back on his shoulders, lifted him over backwards so that he sprawled on the dusty floor of the shop, half-unconscious, blood lathering his face.

'Don't overdo it, dope,' warned Nick as Maxie swung back his foot again. 'That'll be enough.'

Bannister moaned, clamped his hands to his face. Whitey moved over, stood over him, leered down and, holding the gun pointing straight at his belly, snarled: 'Gee, I'd like to give it him. The one, cocky flatfoot causing all this trouble!'

'Get them ideas out of your mind, Whitey,' warned Nick ominously.

'Jeepers, creepers! I wouldn't really do it,' said Whitey. But Maxie's brutal actions had aroused the blood-lust in Whitey. I could see malicious hatred glittering in his eyes. Right then he'd have got a grand kick outta putting a bullet in Bannister.

Nick turned back to Tobias. The old man had been watching everything with a hard, tight-lipped expression. 'What about you, Pop?' asked Nick.

'You're way off beam, Nick,' he protested. He licked his lips. 'There was no deal about beating up Jeffrey that way. You're going too far, Nick.'

Nick smiled disarmingly. 'Don't get worried, Pop,' he said cheerfully. 'Jeff's okay. It's all over now. He's had a bang on the sneezer. But that makes his story good, see? And the pain's almost gone now. It was worth it, well worth it. Ask him what he can buy with the century note he's gonna get.'

The kid stopped whimpering, lowered his hands from his face, stared up at Nick eagerly. 'Is that true, Pop?' he demanded excitedly, speaking thickly because of the blood clogging his nostrils. 'Do I get a C note, Pop?'

'Sure, Jeff,' comforted Nick. 'Take it now.' He pulled a century note from his vest pocket and tossed it towards Jeff like it was confetti. It wasn't confetti to Jeff. He scuttled on hands and knees across the floor, grabbed at the fluttering note before it touched down.

'He's happy enough, Pop,' said Nick. 'Now, what about you? What happened?'

Tobias swallowed, glanced at Jeff's bloodied face, shrugged his shoulders and looked back at Nick. 'Just the way Jeff just said it was. I came down, found them grappling on the floor. The cop had that jemmy in his hand, was trying to bash Jeff's brains in. I couldn't stand by and see that happening. I had to stop him some way.'

'How did you stop him?' prompted Nick.

'I always keep a sap here, under the counter,' explained Tobias. 'It's always there, handy in case of emergency. I used that.'

'That's fine,' said Nick. 'Let's see you get it. Let's see you use it.'

Tobias went around the counter, dug down and came up with a black, pear-shaped lump of rubber, which he attached to his wrist by a loop of leather cord. The leaden core to that sap made it a formidable weapon.

Bannister was half-sitting on the floor now, shaking his head to clear it. Whitey was standing over him, half-watching Tobias as he advanced towards Bannister, dangling the sap in a businesslike manner.

Whitey shoulda been smarter. He shoulda known that cop was desperate by this time. No-one lies down waiting to be sapped without making some effort to save themselves.

Bannister shook his head once more, vigorously this time. Then he went into action like a released spring. His legs doubled up, so his knees hit against his chest. Then he was kicking out with terrific force, smashing the soles of his boots hard against Whitey's ankles, kicking his feet clear from underneath him so he hit the floor with a tremendous thud, shaking himself badly and letting go the revolver as his hands automatically went out to break his fall.

I suppose he was a good cop. He'd taken plenty of punishment with that boot in the puss. There was nothing slow about the way he rolled, scooped up the revolver, levelled it and slowly climbed to his feet. There was an ugly gleam in his eyes as he backed away from us, swivelled the revolver from side to side, covering all of us at the same time.

'Now, you monkeys,' he breathed. 'Now you're really for it. Get your hands up, all of you!' He gestured fiercely at Whitey. 'Come on, hophead! On your feet!'

I've seen plenty of guys who've been angry. Bannister was as angry as any I'd seen. There was murderous, red-hot hatred, in his eyes, and his finger on the trigger of that gun was tighter than I wanted to see it. It was Whitey's gun and Whitey always used a hair-trigger. I didn't make any arguments. Almost before he'd finished speaking, my arms were climbing. The others felt the same way. Their arms were climbing, too. And it wasn't only fear that held us. It was knowledge. It was the knowledge that the cop could shoot any of us, and it would be regarded as in the line of his duty. No cop's ever been hung for shooting a guy. Bannister had the law on his side, and the way he looked then, he was ready to use it to his own advantage.

Nick was the only one who wasn't scared. He'd raised his hands above his head, but he still puffed at his cigarette nonchalantly. 'Too bad we didn't catch you cleanly, Bannister,' he drawled. 'I wanted to wrap it up for the Commissioner.' He sighed, shrugged his shoulders. 'It's the same story, though. We heard Pop and his kid yelling their heads off, burst our way in here to help them, and found you with that gun in your hand.'

Nick had a nerve talking to an anger-inflamed cop that way. I couldn't see the lower part of Bannister's face, because it was masked with blood. But I could see his eyes, and they showed the fight he was having not to squeeze off lead.

He breathed deeply, got himself under control, jabbed his evolver towards Maxie. 'Okay, fella,' he rasped. 'You first. Keep your hands above your head, turn around and walk over here backwards.'

He sure was a smart cop. He was taking care of important things first. Maxie was the one who'd relieved him of his .38 Police Special. He wanted that back. And he got it back.

Max was facing us as Bannister, still keeping his revolver levelled, slid his free hand into Maxie's pocket, turned himself into a two-gun man.

Bannister's philosophy musta been an eye for an eye, a tooth for a tooth. The barrel of that Police Special slashed with paralysing force at the nape of Maxie's neck. His eyes rolled upwards, his head went back and his knees sagged. He kinda twisted as he fell, and Bannister's knee was waiting, rocketed upwards, smashed flush into Maxie's face. The gun was ready, too, slashed at him savagely.

Maxie was lucky, because he didn't hover around in a haze of pain the way Bannister had. He went out cold. Unconscious is the best way to be when you've been pistol-whipped.

Bannister breathed hard, flashed a quick glance down at Maxie, who was lying quite still, and then glared at me. 'Okay, dope,' he snarled. 'You guys asked for it. You're next. Over here.'

He was pointing at me. It was strange. I'd been

scared before. But seeing Maxie treated that way knocked all the fear out of me. Instead, I was feeling as angry as Bannister had been a few moments before. My upraised hands were quivering with rage and my head was swelling like it was gonna burst.

'That's it, fella,' taunted Bannister. 'Rush me. That's just what I'm waiting for.' His voice was gloating and he was deadly serious. He'd shoot me down without compunction. I knew it and he knew it. Yet just the same, I was tensing myself, clenching my fists, swaying forward on tip-toe, ready to dive at him, pulp what was still recognisable of his features.

'Take it easy, Joey,' said Nick clearly. His voice was quiet, smooth like silk, and it took all the steam outta me, steadied me down. It was always the same when I heard Big Nick's voice. He could always soothe me that way.

He went on talking, smoothly like silk so I wanted to listen to him all the time. 'Lay off this guy, Bannister,' he said. 'He's got lead in his head. Slug him the wrong place and you've got a corpse on your hands.'

Bannister sneered. 'You want I should turn you guys in without you suffer first! Each and every one of you's gonna get the same as me. It'll be something to brood about while you're in gaol.'

Nick's voice was still smooth, still unconcerned. Yet there was an intensity in it that got over. 'Don't you touch that guy,' Big Nick warned. 'You've got the drop on us now, but I'm warning you. Don't you dare touch that guy!'

Bannister's pulped lips writhed back to show his teeth in a sneer. But somehow Nick's voice seemed to have influenced him. He growled. 'Why should I bother about you? You'll get what's coming to you, anyway.'

Still keeping his two guns levelled, he sidled towards

the telephone. Big Nick said deliberately: 'You're not gonna do any telephoning, cop. You're in a jam. You've got just one chance. Beat it. If you don't take that chance, you're all washed up. We're all witnesses. You're just a cheap crook.' As he spoke, he took a step forward.

Bannister jagged with the revolver. 'Git back!' he snarled. 'Git back!'

'You can't scare me.' said Nick. He was standing there, tall and commanding, with his big black eyes boring into Bannister. Slowly and deliberately, he lowered his arms, let them hang limply at his side. 'You're all washed up, fella,' he said. 'You're finished. You daren't telephone.'

There *was* something about Nick's voice. It carried conviction.

Even though Bannister musta known we couldn't frame him now, the magnetism of Nick's voice influenced him. He made an effort. 'Get those hands up!' he roared. 'Git back!'

'You won't shoot me,' said Nick smoothly. 'You're too good a cop for that. You're not mad enough to shoot me.' He took another step forward.

The advantage of holding a gun on a guy is knowing he's scared of it and will do anything you want so you won't shoot. But you lose that advantage when a guy's not scared and defies you to shoot.

'Git back, I told you!' rasped Bannister, and I could see the sweat standing out on his forehead. Then, as Big Nick didn't move, continued to stare at him with a mocking smile on his lips, the cop got flustered, put down one gun while he cradled the receiver of the telephone in his hand. 'I'll fix you guys,' he muttered. 'Get you down to headquarters.'

Nick said quietly. 'Okay, Max. Take him now.'

He was looking over Bannister's shoulder, and it

was a trick as old as the hills. Yet, old as the trick is, the instinct of human survival is even older. Bannister flinched, ducked and swung around quickly.

Thinking it over, I see Big Nick musta planned every move he made. His three challenging steps in the face of the pointing revolver brought him just within range of Bannister. When he sprang, his hands were outstretched, grasping for the revolver. He got his hands around Bannister's wrist at the same time his shoulder hit him in the chest. They hit the ground together, trolled over and over, struggling desperately like a coupla jungle cats in a fight-to-the-death embrace.

Whitey dived for the Police Special the cop had left beside the telephone. He wasn't happy until he got his hands around a gun-butt. I wasn't thinking about the gun. I was thinking about Nick, scared right deep down inside me in case that crazy cop somehow twisted his gun around and put a slug through Nick's chest. I wanted to be right in there, helping Nick, helping hold down that damned cop; and suddenly I realised Tobias was hanging onto my arm, shrieking in my ear: '*You can't do it. Joey. You've gotta keep out of it. You've gotta keep out of it. Do you hear me? Remember your head, think of your head.*'

The words were like hammer-blows, punching, driving into my brain. It was like Nick was saying it to me. Drumming it into me as he always did, over and over again. 'Keep out of fights, Joey. Remember your head. Don't get your head banged.'

It made me sweat all over. Those words rooted my feet deep in the ground, so I stood there watching impotently as Nick and the cop rolled over and over, struggling desperately, while Whitey stood over them, gun poised ready to smash down the gun-butt when an opportunity presented itself.

It was a mad, desperate fight. And Whitey, waiting ineffectually, was caught off guard for the second time that evening when a smashing kick from Bannister cracked against his ankle, brought him to the ground, moaning and swearing with pain.

Nick had got the upper hand now, was straddled across Bannister's chest, still grasping his wrist and trying to shake loose the gun. Then a swift, sharp punch from Bannister chopped cleanly across Nick's throat. His eyes kinda bulged as he went over sideways, half-choking, but still gamely holding on to the gun hand.

I wanted to wade right in there and help Nick, even though his warning words were hammering through my brain, nailing me to the floor, telling me I mustn't get into a fight. The sweat was oozing outta me and I could feel tears streaming down my face. In a vague kinda way, I knew I was calling out his name over and over again. It was almost a desperate shout. '*Nick! Nick! Nick!*'

They were panting loud like animals. The noise of their breathing filled the room. They rolled, smashed into a showcase, brought it down, spattering the floor with glass. I could see blood on the floor, on Nick's face and on the cop's clothes. I kept screaming Nick's name, felt Tobias hanging on to my arm, shouting at me to pipe down. It was hot and the room was getting black and I was crying so much the salt tears were stinging my cheeks.

It came to an end abruptly. It was like the knell of doom. It shattered the silence, shattered the noisy turmoil of the struggling, blasted through the darkness of the room, smashed at my mind like a death-blow.

It was one shot. Just one loud, vibrating shot.

I was weak like jelly. A great fear was in my heart.

My lips began to tremble and I could hear myself whimpering, whimpering like a dog who's lost his master. The others were silent, too, staring at that torn and blood-spattered pair lying amid the debris of the shattered showcases.

My heart was in my head, aching intolerably with the misery and agony born of a great fear and a great loss.

I was whimpering aloud and nobody was trying to stop me. Then there was movement, the two figures on the floor separating, one pushing itself to a sitting position, brushing a bloodied hand across its forehead.

A wonderful joy spread through me. I gulped with happiness, felt myself trembling violently with the sudden relief. He wasn't dead! It hadn't happened. Nick was still alive. The cop hadn't shot him.

The complex pattern of my mind began to whirl around, form itself into queer shapes and rearrange itself in a clear pattern that hampered my relief at realising the cop hadn't shot Nick.

This was bad for Nick. I knew it right away. It was what Nick had always wanted to avoid. A dead cop is always trouble. Trouble that's worse than any other trouble.

And this was real trouble because it made Nick – a cop-killer!

4

Maxie felt too ill to talk. The barrel of the revolver had bitten deep into the ridge of his nose, scooping out bone and flesh the size of a dime. Whitey wasn't so good either, the sensitive bones in his foot badly bruised, maybe smashed by Bannister's heavy patrol boots.

Nick was the only one who wasn't scared. At any rate, he didn't let on he was scared. He acted calmly, instructed Pop and Jeff to get hot water and bandages so he and Maxie could patch themselves up.

Nick neatly fastened a length of sticking-plaster across a deep gash in his elbow caused by broken glass, and sipped at the brandy Pop had thoughtfully poured. 'We all saw it,' said Whitey. 'We'll back you up. It was self-defence. It was the cop who had the gun. You were only defending yourself.'

Nick flashed him a silent look of hatred, hurled his empty brandy glass across the room. It smashed against the wall and, as the broken glass tinkled on the floor, he snarled at Jeff: 'Get me another brandy.'

Tobias said soothingly: 'Don't lose your head, son. That's no way to deal with trouble.'

'I'm not losing my head,' shouted Nick. Then he

kinda got a grip on himself, forced himself to take out a cigarette slowly and light it without letting his hand tremble too much. 'Okay, Pop,' he said quietly. 'I'm taking it easy.'

'You've gotta get this straight, son,' said Pop. 'What're you gonna tell the cops?'

Nick furrowed his brow. 'I dunno,' he said. He took a coupla turns up and down the room, hesitated as he almost stumbled over Bannister's body. He tossed away the cigarette he'd just lit with a savage gesture of annoyance, pounded his fist into the palm of his other hand. 'Why the hell did this have to happen?' he demanded angrily. 'Just the kinda thing I've always been careful to steer clear of.'

'I've got an idea,' said Whitey.

Nick swung around to stare at him viciously. 'You!' he sneered. 'You've got an idea! When did you ever have an idea?'

Whitey scowled. 'Just the same,' he said determinedly, 'I've got an idea.'

Nick stared at him, curled his lip contemptuously. 'Okay,' he growled reluctantly. 'Let's have it. What's your idea?'

Whitey nodded towards me. 'The dummy did it,' he said. 'That's easy, ain't it? The dummy did it. He's stoopid. He's crazy. Doesn't know what he's doing.'

The nerve of that Whitey, looking at me that way, saying those kinda things about me! I could feel my head swelling and the slow beating in my brain that warned me it was gonna happen. They were all staring at me – Pop, Whitey and Nick. Nick staring with a speculative look in his eyes.

'It's a cinch,' said Whitey. 'You know the way he is. You've just got to say he's a dummy. He is, too. He's a dope. He's nuts. We tried, but we just couldn't stop him doing it.'

The hammering was in my head like the beating of a war drum. It was starting now. I couldn't stop it. The sweat was bursting out all over me, and I was scared they'd taken my gun from me. Nick's eyes were still looking at me speculatively, wonderingly.

I wasn't worried about Nick now. I was worried about my gun. I was afraid they'd taken it from me, sneaked up on me when I wasn't looking, stolen it from my pocket. I was dripping with sweat now, could feel it running down my legs. And it wasn't in my pocket! I felt for it, plunged deep down in my pocket, fumbling frantically, desperately, knowing I'd die if I couldn't find it.

And the sweat was running out of me, drenching me through and through and I couldn't find it and I was going crazy, feeling madness sweeping over me.

I found it!

It was in my other pocket. I sighed with relief as my fingers slipped around the smooth, comforting butt. Suddenly I was drained of strength, empty and weak like a paper bag that's been busted. I drew the gun out of my pocket, stood staring at it, noticed my hand was trembling badly. Then I pointed it at Pop, got his face lined up between the sights.

Nick's quiet voice said: 'That's not the answer. We don't want any part of this. We mustn't be connected with it. It didn't happen here. It happened way out of town. We don't know a thing about it.'

Pop was staring at me through the sights. His eyes were brown, soulful and sad. I wasn't gonna like shooting Pop. But he was there, framed in the sights of my gun. There wasn't gonna be any alternative about it.

Pop was gonna be shot.

'Can I shoot now?' I asked.

'None of us are gonna know anything about this,' Nick said. 'When Bannister was shot, it wasn't in this neighbourhood. It was way out of town. Remember that, you guys. He was shot way out of town. We know nothing about it.'

I still had Pop lined up. I was anxious to shoot now, my finger twitching on the trigger. 'I wanna do it, boss,' I called. 'Can I shoot him now?'

'Somebody had to have a reason for shooting him,' said Whitey. 'Cops don't get shot for nothing. There has to be someone who's got a reason.'

Nick's eyes narrowed. 'Sure,' he said. 'Someone did have a reason. Randy Regan had a reason. Let the cops worry him for a change. And just to make sure the cops know Randy did it, we'll carve his initials on the cop's forehead.'

The red mist was coming up, engulfing me. I was sweating again, my hand trembling so it was hard to keep Pop focused between the sights. 'Please, Nick,' I pleaded. 'Can I shoot him now?'

'Sure, sure,' said Nick absently. 'You can shoot him now.'

I sighed with relief, squeezed the trigger and heard it click on the empty chamber. I relaxed then, let my arm fall to my side and watched the red mist dissolve together with the rushing sound in my ears.

'How're you feeling, Joey?' asked Nick kindly.

'I feel fine,' I said weakly.

'Put your gun away, huh?' He crossed over to me, patted me on the shoulder. 'You feel good, don't you, Joey?'

'Sure,' I said. 'I feel good.'

'Put your gun away, then.'

I put the gun away.

'You feel better than you've ever felt before?'

'Sure, boss,' I said. 'I feel real fine.' I did, too. Nick always made me feel that way. How could you help loving a guy like that?

'I want you to do something for me, Joey,' he said. 'Something special. I wouldn't want anyone but you to do it for me.'

My chest puffed out. That's just the kinda thing I love doing. Something special for Nick. Something he preferred me to do instead of other folk.

'Sure, boss,' I said proudly. 'Anything you want.'

He thumbed towards Bannister. 'That guy got himself shot,' he said.

'I know,' I told him.

'We've gotta get rid of him, Joey,' he said seriously. 'We've gotta dump him on the outskirts of town. We've gotta leave him there. We don't want any evidence around connecting him with us.'

'Sure,' I said. 'I understand.' I did, too. It was as clear as daylight. He didn't want any part of a cop-killing.

'Got a penknife, Joey?'

'Sure,' I said brightly. 'I know what you want. You want fine to carve Randy Regan's initials on him.'

'You've got it, Joey,' he said. He slapped my shoulder encouragingly, squeezed my arm. 'You're a good guy, Joey,' he said.

I felt all warm and happy inside. 'You want I should go now, boss?'

'That's the idea, Joey,' he encouraged. 'Whitey will help get him into the car; then you're on your own, Joey. And don't let anybody see you.'

'I won't, boss,' I promised happily. 'You leave me to handle this.'

5

It was the next day when Big Nick got the phone call from the Police Commissioner. We had to do things the right way. It wouldn't do for the Police Commissioner to go visiting Nick. So Nick went along to the Commissioner's office, just like any other ordinary guy who's been told to come along for questioning.

Nick took me with him. I knew he took me because he liked to have me around; Maxie and Whitey were jealous about it. They said it was on account Nick didn't want the Commissioner to see Maxie's mussed-up puss.

But I knew different.

The Commissioner had a swell office. It was as big as a pool room, covered with a thick carpet you had to wade through. The furniture was gleaming, polished mahogany, and his desk was massive, bearing three telephones, a large virgin-white blotting pad and three trays of official-looking files tied with blue raffia tape.

As soon as the uniformed cop announced us and closed the door behind us, Nick began to chuckle.

The Commissioner was a lean, middle-aged guy,

with an almost bald head, waxed moustache and thick, bushy eyebrows.

'Sit down, Nick,' he invited, with an anxious look in his eyes as though he was worried Nick wasn't gonna be comfortable there. He dug down in a desk drawer, came up with a new box of cigarettes, which he opened hurriedly, placed ready at Nick's elbow. Then he dug down in another drawer, fished out some glasses and a bottle of bourbon.

Nick seated himself, easily, lazily. I took another chair close by, sat hunched forward on the edge of it, listening intently to everything Nick was gonna say.

Nick chuckled softly. It was a mocking kinda chuckle.

'What's so funny, Nick?' asked the Commissioner anxiously.

Nick looked around the room slowly, flicked ash from his cigarette on to the thick carpet. 'This place.' he said. 'You sitting up here with a set-up like this, an income from Government and ordering me here like I'm a little punk that has to run when you snap your fingers.'

'You know how it is, Nick ...' began the Commissioner.

'Sure, sure,' said Nick. 'I know how it is. You've gotta do things the right way, uphold your position.' He chuckled again. 'It kinda amuses me, though. You having all this and being dependent upon me for it. Knowing if it wasn't for me, you'd be out on your ear '

Nick spoke the last sentence so pleasantly and so easily it wasn't possible to tell if it was a casual comment or a threat. The Commissioner's eyes stared into Nick's. It was the Commissioner who broke first.

He looked down at the bottle of bourbon, reached for it with a nervous hand, asked jerkily: 'Straight or soda?'

'Straight,' said Nick.

He poured three fingers, pushed the glass across the desk towards Nick. He filled another glass, pushed it towards me.

Big Nick said quickly as I reached towards it: 'Joey doesn't drink, Commissioner. Count him out this round.'

I looked at Big Nick looked at Nick reproachfully, shrugged my shoulders unhappily as he shook his head at me, let my hand fall back to my side.

The Commissioner stared at me, looking at Nick meaningfully. 'How's he doing?'

The anger glowed in Big Nick's eyes. 'Who're you talking about that way?' he demanded harshly. 'What d'ya mean, how's he doing?'

The Commissioner was white, worried and flustered. 'I didn't mean nothing, Nick,' he protested. 'I just asked …'

'Just watch your tongue,' warned Big Nick, ominously.

The Commissioner may not have watched his tongue. But he certainly looked as if he was doing his best to swallow it. I felt all good and warm inside. Nick always made me feel that way. Fending off guys who tried to make me feel bad.

The Commissioner sat down, spread his hands on his blotting pad and stared steadily at his copper inkstand.

'Nick,' he said. 'I've got trouble.'

'We've all got troubles,' said Nick easily. He blew smoke-rings with charming unconcern.

'This is serious trouble, Nick,' said the

Commissioner.

'All trouble is serious, Commissioner. Haven't you learned that yet?' Nick still blew smoke-rings. Trouble didn't worry him any.

'This is real bad trouble, Nick. It's a cop-killing.'

For just a coupla seconds it looked like Nick was frozen. Even the smoke-rings seemed momentarily to hover and stop drifting upwards. Then his face hardened as he twisted around his chair to face the Commissioner squarely. In an instant he'd changed from a pleasant, easy-going conversationalist into a hard, seriously perturbed business man. 'Did you say a cop-killing?' he said ominously.

'That's right, Nick,' faltered the Commissioner, like he was scared to repeat it. 'One of the fellas on our force. Got himself a bullet through the chest.'

Nick stared at the Commissioner like the whole world was coming to an end and the Commissioner was to blame for it. Then he stood up slowly, deliberately ground out the stub of his cigarette on the highly-polished wood of that beautiful table. 'You've said it. You've got yourself real trouble, Commissioner,' said Nick. You could see him fighting the anger inside him.

'That's why I had to see you,' said the Commissioner weakly.

Nick said quickly: 'Now justa minute, Commissioner. I'm keeping out of this. I'm having nothing to do with it. It's your baby, you handle it.''

The Commissioner's eyes were wide and startled. 'But what I want ...'

'I don't care what you want,' interrupted Nick heavily. 'Cop-killings mean trouble. Just make sure you handle it the right way.' He glanced around the room meaningfully. 'You've got plenty of reason for handling it properly. Make sure you don't slip up.'

'Nick. Just let me ...' began the Commissioner desperately.

Nick ignored him, took a couple turns up and down the room, talking all the time. 'We've got a sweet set-up. Now we get this dumped in our laps. A cop-killing! How d'you get that way? Can't you run this town straight? It should be easy enough. You've got me doing all the thinking for you.'

'Nick. You've gotta listen,' interrupted the Commissioner. 'The cop was Bannister. He's the cop with family connections in Washington.'

Nick stopped pacing, turned back to face the Commissioner. His face was like a thundercloud. 'Couldn't you have looked after that guy better?' he snarled. 'You knew he was heading for trouble. A guy sticking his neck out that way was sure to get the chopper. You should have foreseen that, looked after the guy.'

The Commissioner's face was haggard. 'Nick, I just want to ask you one thing. Did you ...'

Nick interrupted him once more. 'You've gotta find the guy that did it, Commissioner. The chances are it was one of your own men, fed up with the way Bannister was causing everyone trouble. It was a crazy thing to do, and the guy who did it has gotta take the can back.'

'Nick,' persisted the Commissioner. 'I've gotta ask you this straight. I've just gotta. Did you – did you – arrange it?'

Nick stared at him, eyes widening incredulously. 'Me? Me bump off a cop? Are you crazy?'

The Commissioner swallowed hurriedly. Nick

was so outraged at the suggestion, he'd got the Commissioner convinced.

'I just thought …' faltered the Commissioner. 'Bannister was a pain in the neck and …'

'Wait a minute,' interrupted Nick, as though an idea had just occurred to him. 'Where is this guy Bannister, anyway?'

'They've got him in the morgue. Found him on the highway a coupla miles outta town early this morning.'

Nick was deep in thought, rubbing his chin. Quite automatically he seemed to take over control. 'I tell you what you do,' he said. 'You fix it so Bannister had a shooting accident on the practice range. Get one or two reliable cops to testify. That'll save trouble all round.'

The Commissioner was white-faced. 'We can't rig anything, Nick,' he said. 'It's gotta come out.'

'Why has it got to come out? The newspapers aren't on to it. It happened this morning. They'd have plastered the streets by this time.'

The Commissioner's face was lined and haggard. 'They would have done if I hadn't taken care of it. The two guys who found Bannister wanted a quick buck. They phoned the cops first and the newspapers afterwards. We've got three reporters in the cells downstairs now and they're raring to go. I charged them on technical grounds of obstruction. But I've gotta let them loose, Nick. There's not just one of them. There's three of them. We can't keep them all quiet.'

I saw tiny muscles at the side of Nick's temples tauten. I knew he was furious at this piece of news. But his face didn't show it. He shrugged his shoulders. 'Okay, then,' he said. 'The story's gotta come out. I just feel sorry for you, Commissioner.'

'I'm worried, Nick. What'll I do?'

'There's only one thing you can do. Find the guy who did it and hang it on him. Find him so quick the Feds won't even bother to come over and look around. Your fellas oughta do some police work sometime. Haven't they got any leads they can follow up? Can't they find a fall guy?'

'There was one lead,' said the Commissioner slowly. 'Whoever shot Bannister carved the initials R R on his forehead with a penknife.'

Nick's eyes narrowed. 'Randy Regan,' he said softly. 'Surely he wouldn't have been dope enough to …'

'It was just possible,' agreed the Commissioner. 'I've been checking all morning. Had a dozen plain-clothes men on it. Randy's got a complete alibi, and so have his men.'

'He could have hired a torpedo to come in from outta town,' said Nick. 'Did you think of that?'

'But it isn't logical, Nick,' protested the Commissioner. 'Regan ain't as big as you. But he has got a piece of South Side, and like you he wants to run it with as little trouble as possible. A cop-killing is as serious for him as it is for the rest of us.'

Nick shrugged. 'That's it, then. It musta been some other guy. And it's up to you, Commissioner. You've gotta handle this the best way so it causes the minimum of trouble.'

'Nick!' said the Commissioner.

Nick looked him straight in the eye. 'Well?'

'I've gotta think of my position,' said the Commissioner. 'I've gotta do this thing right. I just wanna be sure of myself. That's why I wanted to see you, Nick. I'll string along with you. I just wanna know where I stand. So I'm asking you again. Did you get rid of Bannister?'

Nick stared at him levelly; he shook his head sorrowfully. 'You get the craziest ideas, Commissioner. I'd run a mile from a cop-killing.'

'But it fits in, Nick. He was causing you trouble. Then suddenly ... this!'

'He was causing you trouble, too.' Nick narrowed his eyes. 'Let me ask you the same thing, Commissioner. Did you kill him?'

The Commissioner was startled. He sat back in his chair, horrified at the suggestion. 'Of course not! The very idea is preposterous and ...'

'That's just the way I feel about it,' said Nick slowly. 'And it's all in your lap now, Commissioner. You've gotta handle And for your sake, I hope you're gonna handle it right.'

'I had to see you, Nick,' said the Commissioner. 'I've got it all worked out. This thing can't be hidden. It's gotta come out in the open. I shan't shilly-shally with it. The only way I can maintain my position and help you is by being on the right side. So I've decided the line to take. I'm not gonna wait for the Feds to take an interest of their own accord. I'm gonna write to Washington tonight. I'm gonna invite those Feds over. I'm gonna give statements to the press and I'm gonna insist no efforts shall be spared until the murderer is found.'

I saw that little vein at the side of Nick's temple throbbing again. The Commissioner was showing him the writing on the wall. He could climb down now, tell the Commissioner what had really happened, delay the investigation.

Maybe he had the angles figured, or maybe it was

just sheer vanity. He lit another cigarette slowly, impudently puffed smoke across the table. 'I wish you luck, Commissioner,' he said lazily. 'I hope you get your man.'

We went straight back to the *Devil's Dive*, the nightclub Nick owned. It was a swell joint, patronised by the best of society, and any other sucker who could afford to spend five hundred bucks on an evening's entertainment.

Nick was deep in thought all the way back, didn't say one word to me. I ran the car down the ramp to the garage beneath the nightclub, reversed it so it would be ready to go out again and crossed to the private lift that took us up to our apartment over the nightclub.

It wasn't until we got into Nick's private sitting-room that he spoke. 'Get Maxie. Get Whitey,' he ordered brusquely.

Maxie was soaking in his luxurious black-and-white-tiled bath. He was in an ugly mood, upset about his broken nose, which was covered in plaster, and the two black eyes that would prevent him appearing in public for a few days. He growled he'd be along in a minute, and I went along to stir up Whitey.

It was the wrong time for Whitey, too. He'd got out the hypodermic and his little capsules of dope, all ready to give himself a shot. 'Can't Nick wait?' he groaned.

'He says you're to come right away.'

Whitey sighed, put the hypodermic away in his drawer. He'd been an addict for years, wasn't satisfied with an under-the-skin injection. He always main-lined his jolts, dug deep down until he found a vein and squeezed the jolt straight into his bloodstream. That way, it gave him a more exciting jag in a shorter space of time. But to dig down and find a vein he had to have time. He couldn't rush a job like that.

When we got to his sitting-room, Nick didn't waste time. 'Bannister's been found,' he said coldly. 'The Feds are coming down from Washington to investigate.'

There was a kinda shocked silence. Whitey gulped. Maxie stirred uneasily.

'We've gotta watch every move we make,' said Nick. He walked across the room, stubbed out his cigarette in a big glass ashtray. We looked at him, kinda dangling in suspense and waiting for what he would say next.

He spoke over his shoulder. 'Check up for me, Whitey,' he said. 'Tobias Slack. Can he be replaced?'

A mean smile twisted Whitey's lips. 'You mean *who* can replace him?'

Nick turned around, flashed him a glance of meaning through narrowed eyelids. It could have been a warning glance, although I couldn't tell what the warning was. 'I mean,' he repeated with heavy emphasis, 'check up on Tobias Slack. *There's only six guys who know who killed Bannister.* Us four here, Tobias and Jeffrey. We've gotta be sure they won't talk.'

Again that meaningful grin from Whitey. 'I get it,' he said. 'I get it. I know the way you work, Nick.'

'Then you know it's smart not to talk too much,' snapped Nick.

Whitey chuckled. It was an unpleasant chuckle. He usually chuckled that way when he looked at me. This time he wasn't looking at me.

'You'd better see Tobias,' said Nick. 'Tell him we'll be along tonight. Tell him it'll be late, when there's no one around.' Again that warning look at

Whitey.

I didn't get any of it. I cleared my throat. 'Tell me what you want done, boss,' I said. 'I'll go see him. You don't have to bother.'

Nick's big eyes watched me gently. 'It's okay, Joey,' he said. 'I'm taking care of it. But you can help me. Go find Sinclaire. Tell him I wanna talk with him.'

I was half way through the door when I remembered that Sinclaire, the nightclub head waiter, wouldn't be on duty for another hour. I turned back.

'I wanna see him now,' said Nick.

'He won't be here yet, boss,' I said. 'He doesn't report for an hour or more.'

'But he may be here already, Joey,' said Nick soothingly. 'Be a good fella. Go get him, if you can find him.'

I knew there were times when I wasn't so smart. I couldn't always remember things and I was slow thinking too. But I was right about Sinclaire. The nightclub was completely deserted. Not even the cleaners had arrived yet. I went back upstairs, was puzzled by the way they all stopped talking when I went in.

'Like I said,' I told Nick. 'He wasn't there.'

'Too bad,' he drawled. He kinda nodded his head at Maxie and Whitey in dismissal. 'That's all, fellas,' he said. 'Now we wait until tonight.'

'You don't have to bother, boss,' I said eagerly. 'I'll fix it.'

'It's all fixed, Joey,' he said. 'You get some sleep this afternoon. You won't get much rest tonight talking with Tobias Slack.'

'Okay, boss,' I agreed reluctantly, just a little hurt he wouldn't let me do the job for him.

'You've got it all straight now?' asked Nick.

He seemed to be talking to the other two, and not to me.

I looked at Nick, puzzled, wondering if I was missing anything.

'Everything's okay, Joey,' he said soothingly. 'Just you get some sleep. Spend two or three hours in bed. Off you go now.'

It worried me. It worried me all the way up to my bedroom. It worried me when I was lying down, so I couldn't get to sleep for a long while.

Whitey's laugh, I mean. The way he chuckled deep down in his throat as I came outta Nick's room. It was like he knew something I didn't.

Tobias Slack looked worried. His son Jeff looked scared outta his life, white-faced and shaking. We stood around in his shop-parlour with the windows heavily shuttered and just one solitary light bulb shining.

'Who else could have known Bannister was here last night?' asked Nick.

'Nobody,' said Tobias.

'You're sure of that?'

'Positive,' he said anxiously.

Nick looked at his fingernails, polished them on the cuff of his coat. Then he inspected them again. 'How about tonight? Who knows we're here tonight?'

'I keep telling you, Nick,' protested Tobias. 'Nobody knows anything about it. There's only us six know you killed the cop ...' He broke off, stared at Nick with a glint of fear in his eyes. Nick was staring at him, eyes hard as black diamonds, his gaze as penetrating as a rock drill.

'What was that, Pop?' he asked softly.

'I mean ...' faltered Pop. 'None of us here knows about that cop-killing.'

'Your memory seems kinda shaky,' said Nick, ominously. 'You seem to be remembering things that didn't happen.'

Pop dropped his head. 'I wasn't thinking,' he muttered. 'It kinda slipped out.'

'Things slipping out can be dangerous all round.' Nick polished his fingernails some more, inspected them and gave a grunt of satisfaction. Then he looked around with the air of just having entered a bar. 'What about a drink, Pop?' he asked. 'These night hours are kinda tiring.'

Pop jerked his head at Jeff, who slipped out to the back of the shop, returned a few moments later with half a dozen glasses and a bottle of bourbon. Nick poured, slowly and carefully, poured three or four fingers of straight bourbon into each glass. Whitey took one, slid another one along the top of the showcase towards me. I reached out for it, and Nick said sharply, 'No. Joey's not drinking.'

'Gee, boss,' said Whitey. 'Let the guy have a drink some time.'

I looked at Nick hopefully. My hand was still outstretched towards the glass. I kinda waited, poised on the razor-edge of indecision, waiting for Nick to say so.

'D'you wanna drink, Joey?' he asked.

Sure I wanted a drink. When my head hurt real bad, that was the only way to stop the pain. It meant I had dreams, nightmarish dreams. But it stopped the pain. I reached out, clutched the glass fiercely.

Nick shrugged his shoulders. 'It's up to you,

Joey,' he said.

I liked the fiery taste of it around my tongue. It trickled down inside me, warm and rosy, radiating electric heat like Nick's words did when he took my part. It was so good, I drained the glass at a gulp, wanted more, noticed Whitey's mean face twisting into a grin as I put the glass back on the counter.

'Want some more, Joey?' he leered.

He knew I wanted more; he was taunting me.

'Here y'are. Help yourself.' Whitey thrust the bottle over to me. I looked at Nick. He turned his eyes away, pretended he wasn't watching, left me to do what I wanted.

I sloshed more bourbon into the glass. From the corner of my eye, I saw Pop kinda half-raise his arm like he was gonna stop me. Nick said loudly: 'Leave him alone, Pop.'

They were talking now, discussing all kinds of things. I wasn't very interested. There was just that warm, rosy glow inside me that made me feel so good. And then, before I'd finished the second glass, everything went wrong. That hammering began in my head. I put my hand to my forehead, held my head on one side to try to ease the throbbing.

There was a kinda hushed silence. I heard Whitey say: 'It got him, quick.'

Pop said: 'You shouldn't have let him. You know what happens.'

Whitey said fiercely: 'Look at Pop, Joey.'

I looked at Pop. He stared back at me, frail, white-faced and now looking just a little scared.

'You're a dummy,' sneered Whitey, and he was deliberately being that way to me again.

It was bad, because my head was already

hammering. I kinda froze, waiting for Nick to say those nice, soothing words. But Nick couldn't have heard him, he didn't say a word.

'You're a dummy,' sneered Whitey. 'You're a prize dope. Look at Pop, you nut. Keep looking at him, you dope.'

It was happening. I couldn't stop it. The hammering and the flush expanding inside my brain. I was trembling all over, and now the sweat was coming, pouring out of me, soaking my clothes, so that when the fear hit me, it was like I was wet all over. I was scared it wasn't there, fumbled for it desperately, knowing they'd sneaked up on me and taken it, and knowing too that if I didn't find it, I'd die. I just had to find it. If I didn't find it, I'd die. Die! Die!

The relief as my hand closed around the butt was so great it made me weak all over. But just the same, I had to get it out. I had the strength for that. I levelled it, trained it so I could see the centre of Pop's forehead lined up squarely between the sights.

'Dope,' sneered Whitey.

'Can I shoot him now?' I asked Nick.

Nick didn't hear me. 'It gets kinda monotonous,' he said to somebody. It coulda been Tobias he was talking to. It coulda been me.

'Can I shoot him?'

'See what I mean?' said Nick. 'Just as soon as Whitey starts shooting off his mouth, it happens.'

Tobias was staring straight down through the sights at me. His eyes seemed very wide apart, very big. I wasn't sure, but I thought his lip was trembling slightly.

'Can I shoot him now, Nick?' I pleaded.

'Sure, sure, sure,' said Nick. 'Do what the hell you

like.'

I squeezed the trigger and the gun bucked in my hand. It didn't sound very loud and I wasn't frightened. It was much better than the other times. Much more exhilarating. It gave me a wonderful feeling like I was God, because this time it really happened, the red hole between the eyes and the meaty plunk of lead ploughing into flesh and bone.

I didn't have time to enjoy it properly, because Whitey was yelling again, frightening me once more. 'He's getting away, Joey,' he yelled. 'You've gotta get him lined up in your sights again. Quick! Look! There he is. Over there.'

It was difficult to find Pop, because he was on the floor. Yet he wasn't on the floor either, because there he was, over in the corner, Whitey pointing at him, yelling at me to get him between my sights, yelling at me he was getting away.

But I was too artful and too quick for him. He couldn't get away. I levelled my gun, and he was lined up clearly between the sights. He didn't look the same any more, dark-haired now, long black hair that hung down over his face. He was taller, too; tall and stringy. And I've never seen a guy so scared. His eyes bulged, his mouth open and flattened as he screamed, and there was a satisfying, stark panic in his eyes.

'You dummy,' yelled Whitey. 'You prize dope. You great dummy.'

They couldn't fool me that way. They hadn't taken the gun from me. I was holding it in my hand. I had his face hanging on the end of my barrel, too. I'd show them this time. I'd show them they couldn't steal my gun.

'Can I shoot him, boss?' I asked, thrilling with

excitement at what was gonna happen.

'Sure,' he said. 'Do what the hell you like.'

It was good, it was wonderful! It was like being warmed all over, inside and outside, right down to the tips of my toes and up to the crown of my head. It was a wonderful, complete feeling of exultation and satisfaction. It was like the wiping out of every bad thing that had ever happened to me and being born all over again in the process.

Nick said softly: 'Take it easy, Joey. Take it easy, boy.'

That made it even better, him speaking to me that way, making me feel good, right deep down inside.

'Nobody's gonna take your gun, Joey,' he said. 'You don't have to worry. Nobody's gonna take it. You can put it back in your pocket now.'

It was a tremendous sense of relief. I put the gun back in my pocket and found my hands were shaking. I was shaking too. And I was wet. Soaked through and through, so my clothes stuck to me. The hammering in my head was dying away now, but I felt faint, drained of strength.

'Sit down, Joey,' said Nick. He came over to me, took me by the shoulder. Gee, that felt really good. 'Sit down, Joey,' he said. 'There you are. That's right, boy. Sit down.'

I closed my eyes, relaxed back in the chair.

'You're drowsy, Joey,' he said softly. 'But you'll be all right in a minute. Now just go off to sleep for a minute.'

I didn't exactly go to sleep. Everything was so blurred, so mixed up, it was good not to think of anything at all, just let my mind go blank.

Then Nick was shaking my shoulder, forcing me

on my feet. 'We've gotta go, Joey,' he said. 'Snap out of it, fella. We've gotta go.'

I got up weakly, knew vaguely it had happened again. I was worried about it. I needed reassuring.

'What happened, boss?' I asked anxiously. 'It all happened so quick I couldn't stop it.'

'We've gotta get out of here, Joey,' he said soothingly. 'You did it again.'

I wasn't deeply worried about it. It had happened before, would happen again.

'Was it Pop and Jeff?' I asked.

'That's right,' said Nick soothingly. 'But you don't have to worry about it. You couldn't help it. It's just the way you are. It's that slug in your nut.'

'Sure, boss,' I said. 'I couldn't help it, could I?'

He nodded across the room. Over in the corner was Jeff, kinda hunched up like he'd slipped down and fallen asleep there. Pop was lying not far away from him. I couldn't see his face, but I could see the bulge of his chest and little flecks of blood spattered on his shirt.

'You couldn't help it, Joey,' said Nick soothingly. 'But you mustn't tell anyone about it. Understand?'

'Gee, boss,' I said. 'I wouldn't tell anyone. Honest I wouldn't.'

'All right, Maxie,' said Nick. 'Just look outside. Make sure no-one's around.' He turned to Whitey. 'You take his arm,' he ordered. 'He's pretty weak now. Get him back and in bed.''

'You know what I think?' said Whitey.

'I'm not interested,' said Nick.

'Just the same,' said Whitey, 'I'll tell you. I think we gave him just a little bit too much to drink. Listen, Joey,' he went on. 'You shouldn't drink so much. It's not good for you.'

'I think you've got something there,' said Nick, with a chuckle in his voice. 'You ought to take notice of what he says, Joey. You shouldn't drink so much.'

I didn't believe him, because bourbon made me feel so good inside, so warm and happy. But I didn't say so. I felt too weak to say anything. My belly lurched, was greasy, queasy and revolted.

I leaned against the wall, my shoulders heaving and my eyes watering as I vomited.

'You're gonna be okay now,' said Nick. 'That's just what you wanted. You're gonna be okay now, Joey.'

Everything he told me was right. I could feel it. What Big Nick said was true.

I was gonna be all right, now.

6

The Bannister killing was played up by the newspapers. Every one of them screamed 'COP-KILLING' in banner headlines, painted a picture of a young, efficiently trained cop who, within a few days of taking his first assignment and showing a special diligence towards his duty, had been mercilessly battered and shot by unknown assailants and dumped at the roadside on the outskirts of town from a speeding car.

The story was hot. And the way the newsmongers wrote it up, it sounded hotter. The way they wrote it, you'd have thought ours was the only town in the whole of the States that had a cop-killing. The newsmongers claimed it showed there was a plague spot in the city, a cancer that would slowly but surely strangle the life of the community and terminate in terrible gang warfare, reminiscent of the days of prohibition.

Yeah, the way those newshounds played it up was comical. But there was its serious side, too. Newspapers are mighty powerful instruments of persuasion. If the newspapers kept up dishing out this news the way they were, pretty soon some of the citizens around town might really begin to believe this *cancer* and *vice* story.

Maybe the Commissioner was acting pretty smart at that when gave an interview to the press, said this blot on the town (he meant the cop-killing) must be cleansed away. He said he and the DA would not rest until the murderer of Bannister was brought to justice. He said he was unwavering in his determination, unwilling to leave any stone unturned. He gave the press a copy of the telegram he had sent to the Federal Bureau of Investigation in Washington, requesting special agents should be sent to help the local police investigate the killing.

There were photographs of the Commissioner, too. They took him seated at his desk, dictating the telegram to Washington into his dictating machine. They took photographs of him together with the DA, the cop Captain and a Senator.

The Commissioner looked really determined, standing beside his desk with one hand upraised in violent denunciation of this *'vile murderer.'*

Yeah, he was so good he got me siding with him. Gee, it was crazy, but he talked so good, there was half of me hoping he'd able to find the cop-killer the way he said he wanted.

There was something in the papers too about Pop and Jeff. They'd been shot dead when they surprised an intruder who wanted to rob them. But there was so much newspaper excitement about a cop-killer, there wasn't much type left to spare for Pop and Jeff. The little item about them was tucked away on the back page, where it wasn't easily seen, and it only appeared in the evening edition. The next day, the newspapers had forgotten it altogether.

I was unhappy about Pop and Jeff. I liked Pop. He was a nice guy. Jeff maybe would have been a nice guy too if he'd lived long enough. Yeah, I was sorry about those two. I shouldn't have done it. I knew I shouldn't have done it. Big Nick said I couldn't help it, and what he said was true. It was just one of my ways. Nick said I wasn't to worry about it either, and I always did what Big Nick said.

Nick always knew what was right.

He was right about that cop-killing, for example. He said it would cause trouble. It did.

Almost overnight, everything changed. There was a kinda tenseness in the atmosphere. All the guys in the saloons along Main Street were on edge. You got the feeling they were always on the point of glancing over their shoulders furtively.

Guys didn't talk so much, either, acted kinda sullen, tight-lipped and humourless. Every day, me, Whitey and Maxie made the rounds of the saloons, the numbers offices and the cat houses, collecting the dough and giving receipts.

Usually it was a pleasant kinda transaction, guys handing over the dough with a joke, watching with satisfaction as we counted off the percentage that was kicked back to them.

Now it was different. They were surly, watched us with suspicious eyes, took their commission sullenly, and stowed it away like they felt guilty, felt they were involved in something that wasn't clean.

Maxie said they were all thinking the same thing. They were all thinking Big Nick had killed that cop or had ordered him killed. But there was only one guy who actually said it. It was Petersen, who ran a pool saloon and stocked one-arm bandits that paid off handsomely.

Whitey opened the machines, while Maxie held the big canvas bag ready to collect the flood of nickels that made a glittering cascade. Petersen watched with that kinda tense silence that had become familiar. When the machines were empty, we went through to his office, me, Maxie and Whitey counting out the nickels, stacking them in neat piles until they were all counted. Whitey entered the total amount in Petersen's cash book, got Petersen's signature against it and counted out Petersen's split. The guy looked mean, narrow-eyed, suspicious and contemptuous. He opened a drawer, scooped handfuls of gleaming nickels into it like he wished he hadn't got to touch it.

'What's biting you?' growled Maxie. 'You look like you've got something on your mind.'

'Maybe I have, at that,' said Petersen. He glared at us venomously.

Whitey said softly: 'What's on your mind, Petersen? We're business partners. There didn't oughta be no secrets between us.' There was that mean twist to his lips. I could see it. Surely Petersen could see it. Maybe he did and it didn't worry him.

'Okay,' he said suddenly, like it was all boiling up inside him and had to come out. 'You want I should tell you what's on my mind. Sure I'll tell you. I'll tell you what's worrying every other guy in this town, too. Pretty soon, the Feds are gonna be on top of us. There ain't gonna be no peace and quiet in this town. And it's all on account of some guys not having enough savvy to know when they're sitting pretty.'

'Meaning which guys?' asked Maxie, smiling gently.

'Who're you kidding?' jeered Petersen. 'You figure I don't know Big Nick engineered this killing?'

He'd said it.

There was a long silence. Now the words had

escaped his lips, Petersen knew he'd gone too far. He looked kinda hunted, said defensively: 'You guys asked me what was on my mind. I guess you wanted me to tell you.'

Maxie said softly: 'Funny how Big Nick knows everything. He said the guys with no brains would figure he was behind cop-killing.'

'Yeah. That's just what he said,' gloated Whitey, with that mean twist to his lips. 'He said only the smart guys would realise the last thing he wanted was a cop-killing. Only the saps would start talking and making wrong guesses.'

Petersen twined and untwined his long fingers with embarrassment. 'What the hell's a guy to think, anyway?' he pleaded.

'Guys who work for Big Nick have to use their brains. We haven't room for saps,' said Maxie softly.

'And saps have to be taught a lesson,' said Whitey. 'It doesn't do Nick any good if saps talk too much, give false ideas.'

Petersen read the intention in their eyes. He jumped up quickly, backed to the wall with his hands held up defensively and his face twisted with fear. 'Now, wait a minute, fellas,' he began desperately. 'You didn't get it right. What I meant was ...'

Maxie hit him first. It wasn't a hard blow, but Petersen was so scared he doubled up defensively, his face buried in his arms and his elbows trying to protect his belly as he bent over.

I saw the brassy glitter of Whitey's knucks as he raised his fist, smashed it down on the back of Petersen's head. The guy went down on his knees, moaning and still doubling himself into a ball to protect his face and belly.

Maxie and Whitey didn't waste time. It was routine to them. They used their knucks and their feet. It wasn't much more than five minutes before Petersen was lying semiconscious, moaning and doubled up in pain with maybe a fractured jaw, a coupla smashed ribs and a severe case of belly-ache.

Whitey was breathless. 'Maybe now you get the idea, Petersen,' he rasped. 'Big Nick don't like guys trying to hang raps on him. Understand?'

The injured man groaned his understanding.

'Come on, Joey,' said Maxie. 'Grab the money-bags. We've got more work to do.'

It was a coupla days later when I saw the dame again. The mousy little dame, I mean. Nick said it was good for me to take a walk each morning, get fresh air and exercise. It was on the way back, almost outside the nightclub, when I caught sight of her, standing pressed up against the wall, dejected, small and pathetic.

I didn't recognise her, just noticed her and passed on. But she recognised me. Her timid voice drew me up short, pulled me around to face her.

'Mister,' she pleaded. 'Can I talk to you?'

The old coat she wore was dusty like she'd been sleeping out in it. Her face was pinched, her big eyes wearing a gaunt, hungry look.

'What d'ya want, kid?'

'You were good to me the other night, mister,' she said, with a kinda childish eagerness in her voice. 'I didn't think I'd see you again. Now I have, I'd like to thank you.'

I crinkled my forehead. So much had happened during the past few days, I couldn't place her right away. Then the wistful, pinched look on her face jogged in my mind. I grinned at her broadly. 'That's okay, kid,' I said. 'That cop was a big, no-good heel, anyway.'

'The money you gave me,' she said wistfully. 'I don't know what I'd have done without it.'

'Forget it, kid,' I said. Then it began to dawn on me, the old drab clothing, the hungry look in her eyes, her pinched little face. 'What are you doing now, kid?' I asked. 'Are you working?'

'Can't get a job, mister,' she said sadly. 'It's my clothes mostly, I reckon. They're pretty messy. They give a bad impression.'

I dug down in my pocket, pulled out another five-dollar bill. I thrust it at her. 'Here, take this, kid,' I said. 'And cheer up; you'll make out okay.'

She made no attempt to take the money, instead looked up at me. 'Gee, you're kind, mister,' she said. 'But I can't take your money, honest. I can't keep taking money. Don't you know anyone who can give me a job? I'll do anything. Anything!'

She was so pathetic, so childlike, so plaintive, I wanted to do things for her. 'What about your folks, kid?'

'Dead,' she said. Just one word, and the way she said it made her sound like she was dead herself inside.

I scratched my chin thoughtfully. 'Guess I don't know much about jobs for dames ...'

She interrupted me. 'The other gentleman,' she said. 'The handsome gentleman. Would he know anyone who'd give me job? I'd do anything. Anything!'

She meant Big Nick. And she was right about Nick. He was good and kind. He'd help anybody. He'd always helped me, hadn't he?

Thinking of him got me excited. There had to be a

job somewhere around in the nightclub. I thrust the money towards her again. 'Listen, kid,' I said. 'I've got an idea. Now you take his dough, see. See that cafe over there? You go buy yourself a cup of coffee. I'll be back in a little while. I'll see what I can do about a job for you,' I said impulsively. I was so excited at the thought of getting Big Nick to help the dame, I didn't even see her across the road.

Nick was always a late riser. He wasn't in his own sitting-room or in his lounge, so I knocked at the door of his bedroom. 'Who's there?' he growled sleepily.

'It's me, Nick,' I said. 'It's Joey. I wanna see you. It's important.'

There was a kinda muffled grunting noise, a creaking of the bed, and he rasped: 'Okay, okay. Come in.'

He was sitting up in bed, unshaven, tousle-haired, with a red-rimmed, bleary look to his eyes as though he hadn't slept much. Lola was still sleeping, lying face down on the pillow with her black hair splayed out across it and one white arm and bare shoulder showing above the sheets.

Nick yawned. 'What the hell d'ya want, Joey?' he demanded. He was always irritable in the morning, gruff and boorish.

'It's about a dame, Nick,' I said breathlessly. 'I wanna talk about a dame.'

Nick stopped scratching his head, stared at me. Then, like he'd suddenly lost all interest in what I was saying, he turned to Lola, shook her vigorously by the shoulder. 'Hey,' he growled. 'Get up, will ya? Get some coffee brought up, will ya?'

She moved uneasily, half-asleep, half-raised her head from the pillows and then let it flop back again.

Nick half-turned, wedged his foot against her side and thrust. 'Wake up, will ya, you lazy bitch?' he growled. 'Get up when I tell you!'

Slowly, heavily, like she was still half-asleep, she pushed herself into a sitting position, grunted a coupla times and brushed her thick black hair away from her forehead. 'I'm tired, Nick,' she mumbled with her eyes still closed.

'Get up when I tell you,' he growled, and he grasped a hank of her hair, tugged it viciously so she squeaked with pain. 'Now get up!' he rasped.

She sighed heavily, pulled back the bedclothes, pulled her feet up and around so she could sit on the edge of the bed. She was a pretty dame with warm, soft skin. Even where I stood, I could smell her warmness, smell the intimate femininity of her, which had been swaddled in the bedclothes.

'Snap it up!' growled Nick.

She stood up sleepily, yawned, stretched herself luxuriously. She stood on tiptoe, arched herself beautifully with arms extended. She fascinated me. What especially fascinated me was seeing her that way – uncovered.

'Okay, Joey,' said Nick. 'Don't get ideas.'

I couldn't take my eyes off her. 'Gee, Nick,' I said breathlessly. 'She's beautiful, ain't she? I like looking at her. She looks so good.'

Lola turned her head, her blue eyes staring at me over her white shoulder. They were icy eyes, contemptuous and disinterested. 'How did *he* get in here?' she demanded. 'Why d'ya have that big-nosed baboon hanging around, anyway?'

She didn't like me. She always looked at me that way, icy-eyed and contemptuous. She always spoke that way about me, too.

'Shut your mouth!' rasped Nick. 'Shut your mouth or I'll close it for good! And get some clothes on, too. Snap it up, will ya?'

Her lips twisted in a sneer. But she knew better than to argue with Nick. She crossed to a chair, picked up a flimsy garment, slipped into it, pulled it up around her loins. Then, as she caught sight of herself in the dressing-table mirror, she poised prettily, arching her smooth body, admiring the softness of her skin and the feminine contours, running her hands over herself like it gave her pleasure.

Seeing her that way gave me a funny kinda feeling deep down inside, like there was something I wanted and didn't understand. I coulda kept looking at her forever. The softness of her skin was pleasant, the smooth roundness of her so fascinating. There was an urge inside me that wanted something. I was like a child crying for something and not knowing what it was.

"Cut that out!' rasped Nick. He was really angry this time. 'Get some clothes on, ya cheap bitch. Can't you see the way he's looking at you?'

Her eyes were still that icy-blue while she looked at me. It was like she was poising herself, proud of her body and wanting me to see it. Yet there was still that contemptuous curl to her lips.

'What's biting you?' she snapped back at Nick. 'There's nothing to it. He don't know what time it is.'

'You've asked for it,' breathed Nick angrily. He pulled back the bedclothes, swung his feet out of bed. His quick movements scared her. She made a quick dart for a chair, gathered up her underclothing.

She shouldn't have got Nick angry that way. He was much quicker than she was. He reached her the same time she reached her clothes. His hand locked in her black hair, jerked her head back, while his other hand slapped, palm cracking flush against her cheeks, bringing a squeal of pain from her.

'Do what you're told, you damned bitch!' he mouthed.

He released her, slapped again, this time with real strength so she reeled over against the wall, hit it hard and slowly slumped to the carpet, holding her smarting cheek and sobbing with pain. Nick's toe prodded the ball of underclothing she'd dropped, hooked it neatly across to her. 'Now get dressed like I told you,' he growled.

With smarting cheeks and eyes glistening with tears, she fumbled among the clothing, tearfully threaded her arms into a brassiere, moulded herself into it, tightening straps, tugging, and all the time giving little sobs.

'Don't take any notice of her, Joey,' said Big Nick. 'Dames are poison. They're all the same. You don't want no trouble with them, ever!'.

'No, Nick,' I said. But I still wanted to look at her. She was pretty; soft and smooth. Nick said I wasn't to look, and what he said was always right. Though it seemed a little strange. If women were poison, the way Nick said, why did *he* always have a dame around? Why did the other guys have them around?

And, no matter what Nick said, I liked dames. They were pretty. They were soft and smooth. They kinda fascinated me. They always made me feel the same, like they was important and meant something I didn't understand. There was that other thing too. A kinda ache deep inside, like I wanted something but didn't know what it was.

'You sit down here, Joey,' soothed Nick. He

pointed to a chair, made me sit so I couldn't go on watching Lola. Maybe it was right what he said about dames. Hadn't she got him angry? I didn't like to see Nick angry that way. His eyes were red and he was breathing heavily. I hadn't done anything, and yet it was like he was angry with me too. It made me feel sad.

'What's this about a dame, Joey?' he rasped.

My mind was all confused now. 'There's a dame,' I said. 'A little dame. She wants a job.'

'So what?' he grated.

'She's hard up,' I said. 'Hasn't got any dough. She needs a job real bad. She'll do anything.'

'You wanna help her?' asked Nick bluntly.

I looked at him happily. He understood. He always understood. 'She'll do anything, boss,' I told him.

'Okay,' he growled. 'I can give her a job in the kitchen or somewhere. Tell Sinclaire I said so.'

It was wonderful the way Nick could always make me feel so happy, so good!

I saw Sinclaire, the staff manager, told him what Nick had said. He pulled a sour face, said he had all the staff he wanted.

'But Nick says you've gotta give her a job,' I insisted.

'Okay,' he sighed wearily. 'Bring her in.'

She said she'd do anything, so they gave her a neat black dress, black shoes and stockings and a chair in the ladies' powder room. It made me feel good she'd got a job like she wanted. And a strange thing had happened to me. I couldn't stop thinking about her. All the rest of the day, I was thinking about her, all the evening too.

Big Nick made it a rule I was never to go into the nightclub while it was open. He said it was on account the customers were a lotta stiff-necks who wouldn't be sociable to a happy-go-lucky guy like me. But I had permission to go around back to the kitchen for my evening meal, and all the time I was there thinking about that mousy little dame with her big brown eyes and wistful little face.

I was thinking about her so much, I realised I wouldn't be happy or able to sleep unless I could see her again.

I hung around the kitchen, waiting for the club to close and the last customer to go. The chef kept telling me it was time to go to bed, but I ignored him, hung around the kitchen while time crawled leadenly like the night was never coming to an end.

I got restless, paced up and down around backstage of the nightclub, until the striptease artist finished her act, came mincing through from out front wearing a broad smile and little else. I knew then I hadn't much longer to wait, because now she was through, the customers would begin to go home.

'What're you doing around back, Joey?' she asked. She put all she had into her dancing. She was breathing heavily and sweat was glistening all over her. Seeing her close up like that gave me that pleasant, tantalising feeling. I kept looking at her, seeing her soft body, smelling her, the hotness of her, the sweatiness of her.

'I'm … just waiting,' I faltered. I was embarrassed, didn't want anybody to know why I was there.

There was a slightly puzzled expression in her eyes. 'You like looking at me, Joey?' she asked, and she said it like she was curious, like a doctor tapping you all over, asking: does it hurt here, does it hurt there?

'You're pretty,' I said. 'So smooth, so soft!'

'You like me, do you, Joey?' There was a curious note in her voice, an enquiring, dissecting expression in her eyes. A waiter with a bottle of champagne under his arm came walking briskly along the corridor, pushed past us, winked his eye as his hand brushed bare shoulders. 'Having fun, Joey?' he chuckled.

'Experimenting,' she called after him. 'Trying to raise a spark.'

They thought I was slow. But I caught on to things sometimes. 'What's that about a spark?' I asked cunningly.

'A spark is something that causes a fire, Joey. Have you ever felt like you were on fire, alight inside?'

I looked at her doubtfully, wondering if she was making fun of me. 'I wouldn't like that,' I said doubtfully. 'I wouldn't like to be burnt.'

She chuckled, moved her body, and it flowed so easily and smoothly I wanted to keep watching her all the time.

'You think I'm pretty, Joey? You like looking at me?'

'Sure,' I said enthusiastically. 'I like looking. You're so soft, so smooth.'

'Wouldn't you like to touch me, Joey? Wouldn't you like to feel how soft I am?'

She scared me. She was nice to look at, but I was afraid to touch.

'Come on, Joey,' she encouraged. 'Don't be shy. Touch me. You can do it if you try hard. Try hard now.'

I tried hard. I reached my hand towards her and it was like something was holding me back. I felt the muscles of my arm draw stiff, refusing to move. I tried to touch her, and the more I tried, the stiffer my arm became.

'I can't,' I croaked. 'You're so smooth, and I can't touch you.'

'It's all right, Joey,' she whispered. 'You don't have to worry. You can do it.' She swayed towards me, the smell of her hotness in my nostrils and the smooth softness of her skin rippling until the warm, soft, smooth roundness of her touched my hand.

The touch of her was a blast of lightning, searing my eyeballs, like a flash of something bursting inside me. I staggered back, felt myself drained of strength and the sweat soaking me through and through. It was hard to get my breath, my chest heaved as I fought to suck air into my lungs. I put my hand to my forehead, swayed.

'Gee, Joey, I didn't wanna make you feel bad like that,' she said. Her eyes were anxious, worried now. 'I didn't know it was that way. I didn't wanna make you feel bad.' Her eyes were moist with worry and concern, and instinctively she moved forward like she wanted to comfort me.

I flinched away from her. I didn't want her near me. I was scared it would happen again. That blinding flash that stabbed me through and through, sapped my strength and drenched me with sweat.

'All right, Joey,' she whispered. 'You won't have to touch me again. You can just look at me. That'll make you feel good, won't it, Joey?'

Yeah, that was what I wanted. Just looking at her. The waiter passed through the corridor again, this time without the bottle of champagne. 'Watch out that spark doesn't burn your fingers,' he warned.

'Leave the guy alone, can't you?' she snapped.

He grinned, brushed against her deliberately in passing.

'You can cut that out, too,' she growled.

He chuckled. 'You're gelling cold,' he said, and touched her again. 'I'll go get the other bead, so you can get dressed.'

She scowled angrily along the corridor after him. I kept well away from her, frightened the blinding flash would slash at me again.

Then she looked back at me and there was sadness in her eyes. 'Dames are not good for you, Joey,' she said. 'You keep well away from them. You do what I tell you. You keep well away from them.'

That's what Nick had told me. He was always right. 'Sure,' I said hoarsely. 'I just wanna look at them. That's what I want.'

'Don't even look, Joey,' she said. 'It might cause you grief. You don't even wanna look.'

I didn't wanna look. Big Nick said I shouldn't. But I couldn't help myself. She minced along the corridor to her dressing-room, with the round softness of her haunches rolling like oiled silk. I couldn't take my eyes off her. When she closed the door of her room behind her, the world seemed suddenly bleak and empty, and I was all of an itch, wanting something and not knowing what it was.

I went back to the kitchen, drank some coffee, and pretty soon the waiters had brought in the last dirty plates. It was time now. The last of the customers had left the nightclub.

The ladies' powder room was furnished real swell, with armchairs, a big gilt-edged mirror, and a thick carpet on the floor. The little dame looked over her shoulder wearily when I entered, and then her eyes widened. 'You shouldn't be in here,' she whispered quickly in an awed voice.

'It's all right,' I said. 'They've all gone now.'

She stood staring at me, fidgeting awkwardly. She looked smart in that little black frock and black silk stockings. 'You shouldn't come in here at all,' she said reprovingly.

'I wanted to see you,' I said. 'I want to know if you're happy.' I was eager to hear her say she was.

Her face kinda softened. 'You've been good,' she said. 'Real good. I don't know how I can thank you.'

'Aw, gee.' I said, flushing with embarrassment and shuffling my feet nervously. 'I just wanted to help you.'

'It was so kind of you. I don't know what I'd have done I if ...' She didn't finish the sentence. Instead, kinda impulsively, she stepped close to me, took my hand quickly, and before I could stop her, she'd raised it to her lips, kissed it.

Nothing like that had ever happened to me before. I stood I staring at her, feeling good and warm inside, the touch of her lips still on the back of my hand.

'I'd got down to my last cent,' she said. 'Don't know what I'd have done without you.'

I looked her over. I couldn't see if her skin was soft and smooth. But she fascinated me. She was so small, so slim, so dainty. It was like I could take her in my two hands and crush her. But I didn't wanna touch her. Big Nick had warned me. It was dangerous to touch dames. Then I remembered. It was nice touching her. There was no blinding flash when she kissed my hand.

I said hoarsely: 'You got everything you want?'

She nodded happily, eyes sparkling. 'They've given me a room of my own, and the food is good.' Her eyes glistened. 'The tips are good, too. I'll pay you back when ...'

It wasn't often Lola came down to the nightclub. This night musta been an exception, because she swept in through the doors imperiously, like a queen, dressed in a vivid red evening gown that reflected a rosy glow over her white shoulders. She brought up dead when she saw me, and then her icy blue eyes switched from me to the little dame. 'You wanna get the sack?' she demanded brutally. 'You know he shouldn't be in here.'

She scared the little dame. Her eyes glazed with the fear of being sacked. 'I'm sorry,' she panted. 'I told him. But he said everyone had gone and …'

'You're new here, aren't you?' interrupted Lola. Her eyes were looking her up and down, icy-blue eyes, hard and contemptuous, scorning the pinched little face, the badly-cut hair and the short nails that made the fingers look stubby.

'That's right, miss.'

'Who hired a scruffy little baggage like you?' The insolence in Lola's voice was like the slash of a whip. The little dame quailed beneath it, bowed her head and said humbly: 'This gentleman here arranged it. He …'

'Gentleman!' Lola gave an abrupt, harsh chuckle. Her eyes flicked to me, made me feel like I ought to be grovelling at her feet. 'You're wasting your time, sister,' she sneered. 'He don't know what it's all about. Can't you tell that just by looking at him?'

The little dame hung her head, hot-faced, said nothing. Lola tossed her head at me, pushed through a far door.

The little dame looked up quickly as soon as Lola was out of sight. 'You must go,' she pleaded. 'You'll get me into trouble.'

'I'll wait for you,' I said eagerly. 'I'll wait for you outside.'

'All right,' she said desperately. 'Anything. Only go now. Please don't make me get the sack.' Her voice was piteous.

'You don't have to worry,' I told her. 'Big Nick said

you can work here.' My chest swelled. 'He's a friend of mine. Nick looks after me. He said you could work here.'

Her eyes were wide. 'He's that tall, handsome gentleman?'

'That's him,' I said eagerly. 'You'll like Nick. He's a fine fella.'

Her eyes shone. He's so handsome,' she said. 'Saving me from that policeman and everything. Just like on the films.'

There came the not-so-distant sound of plumbing working in the prescribed manner. 'Please!' she pleaded. 'Go now. Don't get me into trouble.'

'All right,' I said obediently. 'I'll go.'

'And don't take any notice of what *she* said,' the little dame whispered. 'About the way you look, I mean. She's just trying to hurt you.'

I chuckled. 'She can't hurt me,' I boasted. 'If she hurts me, I'll tell Nick. He'll stop her. Big Nick's always kind to me.'

I waited outside. It seemed a year before Lola came out. She paused when she saw me waiting there, kinda hovered, a glint of amusement in those blue eyes.

'Getting human, are you, Joey?' she sneered. 'Getting a yen for a dame? What next!'

'Go away from me' I growled. 'I don't want to look at you. Nick says you're bad for me. He's right, too.'

She chuckled. 'Just a big kid,' she mocked, and swayed away gracefully, walking like a queen.

The little dame came out a few moments afterwards, turned off the lights and locked the door. She turned to face me with sadness in her eyes. 'Well, thanks for everything,' she said.

'I wanna see you to your room,' I said breathlessly. 'I wanna know you're comfortable.'

She seemed uncertain about it, kinda fought a battle inside herself. 'All right, then.' she said at last, reluctantly. 'You can come along.'

It was a small room at the top of the building. It was comfortable enough, had everything she wanted, including a radio. I looked around, nodded with satisfaction. 'You're gonna like being here.'

'After what I've been through, it's heaven.'

'What's your name?' I asked.

'Sheila,' she said. 'What's yours?'

'Everyone calls me Joey.'

'I'll call you Joey, too. Would you like that?'

The way she said it made my name sound like music.

'Say it again,' I said.

'Say what?'

'My name,' I said eagerly. 'Say it again.'

'Joey,' she said.

It was good to hear her say it. It warmed me through and through. It was so good, I wanted to keep hearing it. 'Say it again,' I said.

'Joey,' she said.

It was wonderful. I wanted to hear it again and again. 'Say it again,' I said.

Her brow puckered, her eyes were sad and pained. 'It's getting late,' she said. 'I have to go to bed now.'

'Say it again, Sheila,' I pleaded. 'Say it again. Please, please say it again.'

She sighed deeply. 'All right then,' she promised. 'I'll say it just once more. Then you must go. Agreed?'

I nodded eagerly. 'Yes. Yes.' Anything just to hear it once more.

'Joey,' she said.

I was happy and sad at the same time. I wanted to

hear her saying it all the time.

'Don't you ever take your hat off?' she asked. 'You're always wearing it, indoors and out ...'

I raised my hand to my head, felt my hat wedged there tightly. 'Nick says I've got to wear it all the time, except when I go to bed,' I told her.

'But that's silly,' she protested. 'Why should he tell you to do that?'

'Nick always knows what's best.'

'But it's silly,' she said. 'Why don't you take it off?'

I hadn't thought about it before. Now she'd given me the idea, I felt the hat irritating me. I wanted to take it off. Yet, I was thinking of Big Nick all the time.

'D'you think it'll be all right?' I asked anxiously.

'Of course, Joey,' she said. 'It can't do any harm.'

'All right, then,' I said with a sudden surge of recklessness. 'I'll take it off.'

Her brow puckered and her eyes half-closed with pained pity as I bared my head. She gave a kinda choked gasp and placed her fingers to her lips. 'Joey, I'm sorry,' she faltered. 'I didn't know ...'

'It don't hurt,' I said. 'No one worries about it. It don't hurt.'

'How did it happen, Joey?' she whispered. 'What was the cause of it?'

I crossed to her dressing-table, stared at my reflection. It was there, the way it always was, like a big vee had been cleaved in head. All around the place it was hairless, the white skin of my skull puckered and wrinkled, the cleavage so deep you could almost bury your fist in it.

'Big Nick said I mustn't talk about it,' I said.

'Put your hat on again, Joey,' she whispered. 'Big Nick was right. You should keep your hat on.'

I liked the way she said Joey. I replaced my hat, asked her pleadingly: 'Say it again.'

Her eyes were so brown and sad when she looked at me. 'What a pity,' she sighed. 'You're such a nice guy. So kind. So much feeling. What a pity it had to happen.'

'Say it again,' I pleaded.

'All right,' she said. 'Just once more. Then you must go.'

'That's right,' I said eagerly. 'Just once more.'

She moved across to the door, opened it up. 'Goodnight, Joey,' she said. 'Sleep well.'

I stood outside her door for a long while after she'd closed it. She was a nice little dame, making me feel warm and happy inside. I was hoping she'd say my name again. But she didn't. That throbbing was beginning inside my head, and I knew it was time for me to go to bed. When that happened, Big Nick told me I should always go to bed.

Funny thing, I didn't dream about guns that night. I dreamed about Sheila.

7

A coupla days later, the Feds came to town. They came in a blaze of glory, the Police Commissioner getting the news boys lined up at the station to meet them. I read the papers after wards, saw the photographs. There were six of them – tall, dark, lean-looking guys with poker faces. There was a picture of the Commissioner shaking one of them by the hand. The Commissioner looked proud of himself, important and acting like owned the town. The Feds were watching him quietly, suspiciously, and the expression on the face of the Fed whose was being shaken made me think it was a banana skin he was holding instead of the Commissioner's hand.

We went about our work as usual, quietly and efficiently. From all over town, reports came in that the Feds were nosing around. But it didn't worry Nick any.

'Feds are concerned with offences against the Federal state,' he said. 'They're not hired to investigate rackets. Maybe they don't like what they see, but it's none of their business. They're just here to get a cop-killer. That's all they're entitled to get.'

I made a point of seeing Sheila every night. It became a habit. I waited outside the powder room until she was through, escorted her upstairs to her little room and said goodnight. She was kind to me, always said my name nicely so it made me feel warm and good inside. Being with her kinda cheered me, made me feel the way Big Nick could make me feel, warm and contented.

One evening not long after the Feds arrived in town, Big Nick told me: 'Get the car, Joey. We're going out.'

I went to the basement, got the car and drove it around front. A little later, Nick came out, looking smart and handsome in his tailored black overcoat, his broad, curly-brimmed black fedora and white silk muffler.

'Okay, get going, Joey,' he ordered as he climbed in beside me. 'The Stewartson joint. Remember that place?'

'Sure, boss,' I said. 'I remember that fine.'

As we were driving along, he said: 'I'm pleased with you, Joey. You've been doing well lately.'

My chest swelled and I felt important. But I wasn't sure I deserved his praise. 'In what way, boss?' I asked artfully.

'You've been going steady the last few days, Joey. You're taking a keener interest in things. You're not getting your ideas so mixed. You know what I mean?'

I thought about it. I did know what he meant. Things had been clearer in my mind these last few days. Events didn't get confused quite so much. I didn't get that hazy feeling so often, thinking I'd been doing and saying things that were silly. 'That's right, boss,' I said. 'I have been getting better. I've been reading the newspapers, too.'

'You're gonna be all right, Joey,' he said encouragingly. 'You're gonna be okay.'

Stewartson owned a pool room down on South Side. The canteen was full of one-armed bandits and juke boxes. It was also a collecting agency for the numbers. When we arrived, one of the assistants was outside waiting for us, ushered us straight through to the office at the rear.

Stewartson had a young guy with him, a tall, fair-headed young fella with a cheerful, turned-up nose. Stewartson said:

'Thought this would interest you, Mr Fenner. That's why I asked you to come on over.'

Big Nick took his time selecting a cigarette from his case, steadily regarding the young man meanwhile. 'Who is this guy?' he asked.

The young fella grinned eagerly. 'My name is Dale,' he said. 'I'm a reporter.'

Nick struck a match, lit his cigarette. 'What paper?'

The young guy looked embarrassed. 'Not any paper in I particular. You see, Mr Fenner, it's this way. When we heard in Washington the Federal agents were down here, I thought it would be an ideal opportunity to get a story. So I kinda fixed with an editor, and he's willing to give full consideration to any story I turn in.'

Nick puffed smoke into the kid's face. The kid jerked his I head back and coughed. Nick said softly: 'That'll be real nice for you, won't it?'

The kid looked at him suspiciously. 'I know everyone thinks reporters are nosey guys,' he said. 'But they're just doing a job. Just like everyone else.'

'Sure,' Big Nick said gently. 'Sure, I understand.'

'Mr Stewartson here said you'd be the best man to see,' Dale added awkwardly.

'He was quite right.' Nick puffed smoke into the air this time. 'What exactly is it you wanted to know, kid?'

The kid said, with boyish enthusiasm: 'It's this

way, Mr Fenner. I've been looking around the town. Seems there's not much that's illegal you can't do here. Numbers, pools, racing, nickel machines – all being run openly before the very eyes of the police.'

'Anything wrong with that?' asked Nick.

The kid stared at him. 'It's illegal,' he protested. 'The State ordinance specifically forbids the use of gaming machines.'

Nick looked at Stewartson. Stewartson said heavily: 'I asked the Police Chief if he'd be kind enough to step along and see Mr Dale.'

Nick nodded approvingly. 'What could be better?' He blew more smoke towards the ceiling. 'You'd like to see the police chief, wouldn't you?'

The kid didn't like it. He could sense something wrong. But he couldn't put his finger on it. 'Sure,' he said hesitantly. 'I'd like to see the Chief of Police.'

Stewartson kicked a chair across to him. 'Might as well be comfortable while you're waiting.'

Nick picked up the telephone, inspected his fingernails as he waited to get through to the *Devil's Dive*. 'I wanna speak to Maxie,' he said softly. A few moments later, he added: 'Some urgent business has turned up, Maxie. I want you and Whitey to meet me here. You'll see my car outside Stewartson's joint.'

That was all. Nick hung up then, sat on the edge of Stewartson's desk to wait for the Police Chief, all the time staring at young reporter. The kid couldn't return Nick's stare. It was as though Nick's eyes were wearing him down, breaking him down, bit by bit, spreading him in little pieces all over the floor.

The Police Chief took his time getting over. It must have been all of five minutes before he arrived. He saluted Big Nick, nodded to Stewartson and then stared at the reporter curiously.

'I want you to meet Mr Dale,' purred Nick. 'He's a reporter. A freelance reporter. He's trying to get a story for a Washington paper. Probably one of the syndication companies. Mr Dale figures there's a lotta vice going on in this town, wants to write it up, expose it all. That's the general idea, isn't it, Mr Dale?'

The kid was liking it less and less. He still wouldn't look at Nick. Instead, he looked at the police captain, licked his lips nervously. Then he kinda squared his shoulders, jutted with his chin. 'That's the way it is, I guess,' he said, almost defiantly.

'He figures this town is a den of iniquity,' chuckled Nick.

'Is that so?' asked the Police Captain. He sounded genuinely surprised.

The kid said angrily: 'What game are you playing, anyway? You know what's going on, right enough. You've just passed through a roomful of nickel machines. Those one-armed bandits are illegal in this State. You're a cop Captain. You ought to know that.'

The cop Captain stared at him steadily. 'You're making a mistake, son,' he said. 'You're seeing things. There ain't no illegal machines working in our town.'

The kid got to his feet, his white face trembling with indignation. 'They're right outside this very door,' he protested. 'You can't deny it. They're right under your very nose.'

'You're seeing things, kid,' said the cop Captain. He smiled smoothly. 'You ought to go back to Washington, son. Get yourself a job peeling oranges.'

The kid breathed hard; it was all he could do to contain himself. Then, without a word, he spun on his heel, strode out of the office.

Nick said to the cop Captain quickly: 'You won't see him again. Ever! Play it the right way.' Then he was striding after the kid, rapidly overtaking him, catching him by the shoulder, twisting him around.

'Easy, son,' he said. 'You oughta make your way around more slowly. You don't get anywhere by sticking your neck out.'

The kid said hotly: 'You're in this just as deep as they are. I know your type!'

The soft smile almost left Nick's face. His eyes glinted dangerously, but his voice was as smooth as silk. 'You wanna convince those folks who are gonna read your page, don't you, kid? What about some photographs? You can get some pretty slick photographs of folks operating these nickel machines.'

The kid said: 'I've got all I want. I've got proof enough. Unconsciously his hands moved towards his jacket pocket, jerked back as though he suddenly remembered he shouldn't reveal where he kept those pictures.

'You've got it all wrong, kid,' said Nick. 'I'll prove it to you. I'll take you straight down to the Police Commissioner's office now. You talk to him for yourself. Tell him what you think. Hear his story.'

The kid didn't realise it was a bribe. I could see his eyes shining as mentally he wrote that article, describing how the Police Commissioner himself had denied there was illegal gambling in the town while it was there for anyone to see. The kid was greedy for that story. His eyes were glistening. 'I'll take you up on that,' he said quickly.

'It'll be a pleasure,' said Nick.

When we got outside, I climbed into the driving seat, Nick climbed in beside me and the kid opened the back door of the car. Maxie and Whitey moved out from the shadows so quickly and quietly the kid never saw them. As he was poised with one foot in the air, Maxie hit him from behind, bundled him inside the car and followed after, slamming the door behind him. Whitey was around the other side, piling in, using his knucks and the butt of his gun, sandwiching the kid so he couldn't escape.

'Take it easy,' said Nick casually. 'Don't mush him up too much.'

There was the sound of laboured breathing from behind us. 'He's out,' said Whitey. 'Like a baby. Just one sock on the chin and he was out like a light.'

'Get going, Joey,' instructed Nick. 'Take a little run around the park.'

The park was on the extreme south side of town. It kinda blended naturally into the country, so you couldn't tell where the park ended and the country began. The main highway through the park was lighted, but the other roads were tree-lined and dark. Nick directed me, and finally I pulled up in a deserted spot by the side of the boating lake. On account of it being so late, there was nobody around.

'This'll do,' said Nick.

Whitey and Max bundled the kid out of the car. He fell on lands and knees, kinda groaned, and then squealed with pain.

Maxie grabbed him by the hair, jerked him to his feet.

'Frisk him,' ordered Big Nick.

He hadn't much in his pockets. A wad of dough, which Whitey tucked away in his own pocket, visiting cards, the usual odds and ends a guy has in his pockets, and a roll of undeveloped film.

Nick took the film, opened it up, held it in the flame of his cigarette lighter so that, as it spurted with flame, it illuminated the kid's terror-filled eyes and bloodied face.

'I guess you did it all wrong, kid,' said Nick.

The kid's voice was so shaky he could hardly get the words out. 'Did you … did you mean … I'll forget all about it, Mr Fenner? Honest I will. I wish I'd never thought of the idea and …'

'You made one mistake,' Nick said levelly. 'You thought of the idea. That was your mistake.'

'But I promise I won't …' the kid began desperately.

'The lake's the best place for him, Max,' said Nick casually.

'It isn't more than two or three feet deep,' Whitey protested.

'So what?' said Nick. 'Fix it so he can't swim.'

'That's easy enough,' said Maxie. 'Give him another faceful of knucks.'

'He's caused us trouble,' Nick said softly. 'Prod him around a little first.'

Hearing Nick speak that way sent a cold shiver down my spine. It didn't seem to have that effect on Maxie. He gave a kinda chuckle. Seconds later, I heard Whitey's dry, hard chuckle.

'Don't take too long,' called Nick. 'It's getting kinda late.'

I felt sick when I heard them chuckling that way. Maybe there was something happening to me. Maybe I was seeing things more clearly, and it might not be good for me. I'd never felt this way before. I felt sick, didn't wanna watch as they bundled the kid away into the darkness. I didn't wanna hear when he let loose a high-pitched shriek of agony that dwindled into a mumbling, protesting, inhuman moan. It took a long while.

'What's the matter, Joey?' said Nick. 'Don't you feel good?'

'No, boss,' I told him honestly. 'I don't like it. It's making me feel bad.'

'Nonsense, Joey,' he soothed. 'You never took bad before with things like this. You've got jumpy. You just gotta get used to it. You've gotta steel yourself. Try it now. Steel yourself. Go see what's going on.'

I didn't wanna see, but Nick's voice was so soothing that I couldn't resist him. The kid was a kinda misshapen lump, lying there whimpering and moaning like some sub-human being, his limbs splayed out at awkward and obscene angles.

'He was tougher than I figured,' said Maxie. He was sweating.

'I figured it would be easy,' said Whitey with a note of surprise in his voice. 'A guy goes out on a cold day, trips, falls, and bingo – he's got a busted leg. As easy as that.'

Nick said: 'Snap it up! There's things to do.' There was a kinda greedy note in his voice. He stirred the misshapen, whimpering bundle with his foot. 'Too bad the kid didn't learn it doesn't pay to be too clever.'

Maxie bent, dragged the kid to his feet. The kid shrieked with agony, even though he musta been half-unconscious. Whitey helped Maxie, and together they dragged him to the edge of the pool. They held him for a moment, then let him go. Gently he eased forward into the water without a splash, barely making a ripple.

Like Whitey said, it was only two or three feet deep there. The kid went right under. He went down like a stone, no frantic flurry of limbs, just little bubbles that slowly formed on the surface of the moon-flecked water.

We waited maybe five minutes, and that was long enough, because no guy can live and breathe in water for more than five minutes.

'Okay,' said Nick. 'That's good enough for tonight.'

I still felt sick when I climbed back into the driving seat. Now it was all over, Maxie and Whitey were a little quiet, like they weren't so happy about it. Nick sensed their silence, glanced over his shoulder. 'I know just the place to warm us up, fellas,' he said.

Whitey grunted.

Nick said: 'Drive to Madame Rozetti's, Joey.'

Maxie said: 'I'm gonna like that.'

When we reached the cat house, there was an argument going between the usher and a young guy who had a little doll with him. The doll was so stewed, she couldn't stand without help, couldn't keep her eyes open. She was just a kid, maybe eighteen, maybe less. The guy with her had been hitting the bottle, but did at any rate have his eyes open.

Madame Rozetti thought it was a business call, beckoned us to go through to her own, beautifully furnished private room.

Maxie grinned, shook his head. 'Not tonight, lady,' he said. 'This is our night on the house.'

Madame Rozetti chuckled, fluffed up her hair so her bejewelled fingers sparkled in the light. 'You know my girls. Which ones you wanting?'

Maxie said quickly: 'Bright-eyes for me. Is she free?'

Madame checked in a ledger she had on the

reception desk. 'You're lucky, fella,' she chuckled. 'You know the way - Room 28.'

Whitey had that mean twist to his lips. It gave him sadistic satisfaction to know the girls hated him, tried every way they knew to avoid being with him. He went with the same way as he did everything, with his mean, twisted streak of cruelty well to the forefront.

'I'll take a gamble,' said Whitey. 'Run your finger down the list. Give me the first one you come to who's free.'

Madame sighed. 'Room 12,' she said. 'It's Elisia again.'

The twisted grin on Whitey's lips was even more cruel. 'I bet she hasn't forgot me from last time.'

I didn't understand what kick they got from going with dames. It always bored me going to the cat house. I just had to sit around and wait for the others.

Nick was looking across the room with a puzzled frown on his face. The young guy had given up holding the little dame on her feet. She was slumped in a chair, legs askew, skirt rucked up and head hanging.

Nick jerked with his thumb. 'What's the trouble there?' he demanded.

Madame shrugged. 'Coupla drunks,' she said. 'The guy's picked up the kid somewhere. Now he's got her stewed, he wants somewhere to park.' She snorted indignantly. 'We don't do that kinda thing here. It gets bad for business if we allow guys to bring their own dolls.'

The usher seemed to agree with the young guy. The kid swayed over to the desk, the usher holding him gently by the arm.

'I told you to get him outta here,' snapped Madame.

The usher said: 'It's okay. He's booking himself a dame.'

Madame nodded towards the little Jane asleep in the chair. 'What about her?'

'She's waiting down here,' explained the usher. He chuckled. 'She's in no state to go anywhere, anyhow.'

'It'll cost you ten bucks,' Madame told the kid.

The kid swayed, dug down in his pocket, came up with a handful of notes. By the time he'd counted out ten, there were only a couple left.

'Show him upstairs,' Madame instructed. 'Room 23.'

I was watching Nick. There was a curious expression in his eyes. He kept looking at the little dame who was asleep. She was a cute little thing. Her flesh was soft and smooth, too. I could see it. The way her skirt was rucked up showed a band of white flesh above her stocking-tops.

It was as though Nick couldn't take his eyes off her, and when the usher had led the young guy upstairs, Nick leaned across the table, whispered into Madame's ear.

I saw her eyes widen. 'Easy up, Nick,' she said. 'You've got all my girls to choose from.'

He said, fiercely and loudly: 'I wanna change. Understand? I know 'em all so well, I can recognise each and every one of them by their ankles only. I wanna change. D'ya understand?'

'Have a heart, Nick,' she pleaded. 'She's just a young dame, a good girl. You can tell that. Not one of these cheap little tarts. She probably doesn't know what it's all about, innocent the way she was when she was born.'

Nick's face got heavy and ugly. 'You want I should

get mad with you?' he gritted through his teeth.

'Even if I wanted, Nick, there isn't a spare room.' Madame was pleading with him. 'I've got a girl in every room. You can have any one of them you want. But leave the kid alone. You can't mess up her outlook on life.'

'I wanna change,' said Nick thickly. 'I wanna room too.'

She sighed. 'I haven't got a room.'

'There's your room,' said Nick. His eyes were narrowed as he stared at her. She stared back at him, trying to fight him down. Then slowly her eyes dropped. She nervously twisted the rings on her ringers. 'Okay, Nick,' she said resignedly. 'You can have my room.'

The usher came down and Nick beckoned him over. 'The dame,' he said, pointing to the little doll. He jerked with his thumb. 'Madame Rozetti's room. Make it snappy!'

The usher looked at the little doll, then switched his eyes to Madame. She shrugged her shoulders despairingly, nodded he was to do as Nick told him.

She was like a child, waxen-faced, exquisitely dainty. The usher picked her up in his arms like she was weightless. Her head sagged back and her arms were hanging limply. She sure had hit the bottle. She was out cold.

'Careful with her,' warned Nick. 'Don't bang her.'

The usher grunted, carried the dame through into the back bedroom, which was Madame's special and private preserve.

'Nick!' said Madame.

He was following the usher. He stopped, half-turned towards her.

'She's just a kid. Nick,' she whispered. 'Go easy with her.'

'Aw, shuddup!' he rasped.

It was monotonous sitting there, waiting. Madame gave me the funnies, and I read all the way through it and still none of them had come back.

I yawned, watched a fly on the wall, tried to hypnotise it and make it walk in a straight line along a crack in the plaster.

Then the young guy came down. He looked white and shaky, like he was gonna be sick any time, passed a hand over his forehead, looked around dazedly. Then he looked at Madame.

'Where is she?' he asked.

Madame jerked her head towards the door. 'Gone home,' she said abruptly.

The kid nodded like he half-understood her, staggered blindly out through the door.

A little later, Maxie and Whitey came down. They hung around for a time, decided not to wait for Nick.

I waited.

It seemed hours.

I waited.

Nick came out at last. He jerked his head at me. 'Okay, Joey. Let's go.'

Madame intercepted him at the door, stood squarely before him with her broad arms akimbo. 'What about the dame?' she demanded.

'What about her?'

'You can't leave her here that way,' she said. 'I'm running a business on proper lines. I don't want any trouble.'

'Quit squawking,' he growled. 'I finance your business, don't I?'

'You pay me to make sure it runs without trouble,' she said. 'Leaving that girl here means trouble.'

'Well, get her out of here.' He gestured angrily. 'Get her out of here.'

'It's not my kinda work, Nick,' she said. 'You oughta know that.'

'Get the usher to …'

'He's gone home,' she interrupted. 'The time you've been, you musta half-killed …'

'Okay, okay,' he interrupted. 'Quit squawking.' He jerked his head at me again. 'This way, Joey. Follow me.'

She was such a little doll, and I liked looking at her, because her skin was so smooth and soft. She looked so fragile and china-like. I didn't like to touch her. She was still out cold.

'What're you waiting for?' growled Nick. 'Pick her up, will ya? Take her out back to the car. And don't let anyone see.'

I didn't wanna touch her. But Nick was looking at me, his eyes forcing me to do it, and when I timidly reached out, touched her, she was so cold and white it didn't have that effect upon me. No blinding flash, no sweating.

She was light, like a feather. I held her in my arms, and Nick grabbed up a handful of clothing, balled it together and dumped it on top of her.

Madame screwed up her eyes like she was pained when I came through carrying the little doll. 'You gone crazy, Nick?' she demanded. 'Aren't you even gonna dress her?'

'Keep outta this,' he warned. 'I'm getting her out of here, the way you want. How I do it is none of your business. She's a smart little trick, anyway. She knows how to dress herself.'

She narrowed her eyes. 'Nick,' she said, with black glitters showing through her eyelashes, 'you're the meanest, most selfish and hardest monster of a man I ever met or heard of.'

It got me mad hearing her talk to Nick that way. She was crazy. She had to be crazy. Nick was a good guy. One of the best guys there were. He had to be. Nobody else could make me feel warm and good like Nick did. He was one of the best guys alive. I guess I almost loved him.

But maybe it was a joke. Nick chuckled when she said that. 'Okay, Rosey,' he grinned. 'You've had your say. Watch out it didn't cost you something to get it off your chest.'

She didn't laugh like it was a joke. She just watched us with hard eyes as Nick led the way, opened the door, looked out, beckoned me to follow and opened the door of the car so I could thrust the little doll inside, drop her on the back seat.

'Okay, Joey,' he told me. 'You can ride in the back. I'll drive.'

He drove way out to the South Side park again, stopped at a darkened bench. There was a chuckle in his voice as he said, over his shoulder: 'Okay, Joey. Dump her on that bench.'

She looked all white in the darkness. She was cold, too. Colder than anybody should be. I propped her up on the bench the way he wanted.

'Okay,' he said. 'That's fine.'

'She'll get cold there, boss,' I told him. 'It's a cold night.' Even though I was warmly clothed, I shivered slightly.

He chuckled slightly. 'That's good for her, Joey,' he said 'Ever hear of the Stoics? The strongest people that ever lived. They made themselves that way by sheer will-power and determination. They slept out at nights without clothes or protection of any kind. It was good for them, built them up.' He chuckled again, like he found everything very funny.

'What'll we do with the clothes, boss?' I asked.

'Dump them along the road,' he said.

He drove a long way before he told me to heave her clothes out of the window. We were travelling fast at the time, and they musta been scattered over a long stretch of road. I had to lower the window to drop them out, and the slipstream from the wind was cold so I shivered.

'Gee, that dame must be cold, boss,' I said.

He chuckled. He kept on chuckling. 'Just think of it, Joey,' he said. 'Think how she'll feel when she wakes up in morning, finds herself in the park with no clothes!'

8

It proves what a big guy Nick was, how important and how everybody knew him. The Feds hadn't been in town more than a coupla days before they took the trouble to pay Nick a visit

Nick wanted me, Maxie and Whitey to be present at the interview. Only two of the Feds came. A coupla miserable-looking guys, alike in their grey suits, brown fedoras, and the lean, hungry expression on their faces.

Big Nick was nice to them, I thought. He grinned at then expansively, invited them to sit down, make themselves at home. 'We're sure grateful for having distinguished folks like you among us,' he said pleasantly.

It showed the kind of guy Nick was, big-hearted and kind, making them welcome that way when they could be such trouble to him.

But those men didn't appreciate it. They reluctantly perched themselves on the edge of their chairs, stared at Nick with hard eyes.

It didn't worry Nick any. He was too big for mean-minded little guys like them. He leaned back in his chair easily, relaxed comfortably, smothered a yawn and drawled: 'Well, what's biting you guys?'

'You know what's biting us, Fenner.'

Nick's eyes widened in surprise. 'Now how would I know that? How would I know what goes on in the minds of Federal agents?'

'This is a crooked town,' snarled one of the Feds. 'It's crooked from top to bottom, rotten through and through. The police are on your payroll from the lowest flatfoot on night duty right to the very top one.'

'You don't say,' drawled Nick.

'If we had a guy like you in Washington …' breathed one of the Feds.

The smile was still on Nick's face, but there was an angry glitter in his eyes now. 'What was that?' he asked softly, his voice smooth as silk. It was like he was trying to coax an insult outta him.

The other Fed, the one who hadn't spoken yet, said warningly: 'Hold it, Jake. That's local politics. It's none of our business.'

Jake glowered angrily, uncrossed his legs and crossed them the other way, fumbled in his pocket for a cigarette. He was trying every way he knew to prevent hot words from bubbling out from inside him.

Nick asked, with narrowed eyes: 'Just what is it you boys want?'

'When was the last time you saw Bannister?' asked the Fed.

He was a fine guy, Nick; afraid of nothing. He grinned right into the Fed's face, impudent as hell. 'You mean the poor chap who got himself shot?'

'You know who I mean,' rasped Jake.

Nick said in an aside to Maxie: 'Remind me later, will you, Maxie? Better send a wreath. It slipped my mind.'

Maxie grinned. 'Sure, Nick. You want it should be a big one?'

Nick gave the matter a thought. 'Better make it a small one, Maxie,' he said. 'Quite a small one. He was only a little guy.'

Jake breathed hard. 'I asked you a question,' he repeated in a hard voice. 'When did you last see Bannister?'

Nick chuckled. 'You ask the most stupid questions. I've never set eyes on Bannister. D'you think I go around town making the acquaintance of every dumb flatfoot?'

Jake's face was impassive now. You couldn't tell if he was mad or otherwise. 'I'll lay it on the line for you, fella,' he said. 'A cop's been killed. The Feds have been called in. They'd have been in anyway, so it looked good when they were invited instead of waiting until they came of their own account.'

'You're boring me,' said Nick lazily. He picked up his paper-knife, began to pare his fingernails.

Jake went on like he hadn't been interrupted: 'Bannister was a sound cop. He came from a good family, a family of cops. He was a right guy from the top of his head to his heels. He musta been the one guy on the local force who wouldn't play.' Jake's face was still impassive, but there was a tightening of his throat muscles to show the fury boiling inside him. 'Bannister made himself awkward, Fenner,' he went on. 'Records at police headquarters show that in the few days he was here, he started a one-man clean-up.' He paused, licked his lips. 'It isn't difficult to figure from there on, Fenner. That guy was a good cop. So good, he was a thorn in your side. Then what happened?'

There was a long pause. Nick went on cleaning his fingernails without looking up. Maxie stared at the ceiling and whistled soundlessly. Whitey was reading through a racing sheet, picking the bets he was gonna make.

The long silence continued, waiting for something to happen.

Nothing did happen.

Nick sighed. 'Any time you guys wanna leave, it's okay by me.'

Jake leaned forward, jabbed a bony finger towards Nick for emphasis. 'We know you figure you're sitting pretty,' he rasped. 'There's nothing can tie you in with Bannister's killing.' His voice raised, became strong and vibrant. 'But, it's gonna be done, Fenner. We're gonna hang it on you. It may take a week, a month, or a year. But we're gonna do it, Fenner. We're gonna hang that murder right around your neck, and the world's gonna be a better place for everyone just as soon as we do it.'

I thought Nick would get mad at him talking that way, abusing him. But Nick's such a naturally kind guy he doesn't provoke easy. He merely chuckled. There were imps of mischief in his black eyes as he said: 'That's fine, fellas. I like to see guys who are devoted to their duty. Drop back in a year or so and tell me how you're getting along.'

Jake's hard eyes bored into Nick's. It was like he was trying hypnotise him. He went on staring in that way for what seemed five minutes. But if he figured he could stare down Big Nick, he was mistaken. He musta realised that, because he got up abruptly, jerked his head towards the door, said to the other Fed: 'Come on, Dale. Let's get out of this place. It turns my guts over.'

Something seemed to snap inside Nick. The smile slipped from his face, his eyes hardened and he sat forward, spreading both hands on his desk. 'Watch your foot, fella,' he said ominously. 'You're standing on it.'

Jake eyed him contemptuously. 'You don't scare me, fella,' he said. 'I don't scare easy.'

'Watch your foot, fella,' repeated Nick dangerously. 'You're standing on it!'

It was a funny thing to say. But Nick always used that phrase when a guy got him mad.

Maybe the Fed knew about it. He kinda snorted, strode across the room, pushed out through the door without even looking over his shoulder to make sure the other Fed was following.

Maxie was right behind them, slammed the door as they went through. 'How d'ya like that?' he demanded explosively. 'Coming in, accepting our hospitality and insulting us right to our faces!'

'Shuddup!' snarled Nick.

'Listen, boss. I was only ...'

Maxie should have known better than to argue with Nick when he was mad that way. The inkstand on Nick's desk made a mess when it smashed on the wall above Maxie's head.

'Get out!' roared Nick. His face was red, and he was shaking with anger. 'Get out, all of you! Get out before I get mad!'

We got out quickly. It wasn't often Nick was this way, but when he was, it was better to leave him alone. I didn't mind him losing his temper. Once in a while a guy is entitled to blow his top. Especially a guy who most of the time is as nice as Big Nick. I knew he would be kind to me next time I saw him. He'd pat me on the shoulder, tell me to *Take it easy, Joey,* and I'd get that warm, happy feeling stirring inside me, the way only Nick could make me feel.

Maybe it wasn't only Big Nick who could make me feel good and warm inside. The little dame Sheila could make me feel the same way when she said my name.

I used to wait for her at nights, talk to her a little while, escort her upstairs to her bedroom. That was fine. And then, one night while I was waiting for her, one of the guys in the band stayed late, played the piano. He was a new guy, and he played the piano like he broke his first tooth on an ivory key board.

It was late at night. All the nightclub staff had gone home or upstairs to bed. Sheila was wearing that same little black dress. 'Hello, Joey,' she said.

It was good to hear her saying my name that way. I warmed all over, felt strangely excited.

Her eyes were kinda sad, like she felt sad for me. 'Waiting for me again, Joey?' she said, like she was talking to herself. 'You're old faithful, aren't you? Just waiting like you want me to pat you.'

I furrowed my brow in puzzlement. It was wrong. I didn't want her to pat me. 'Just say my name, huh?' I said.

'All right, Joey,' she said. 'You're a real nice guy.' Momentarily her eyes slipped up towards my hat. 'Such a dreadful pity ...' She broke off quickly, looked away.

'What's a pity?' I asked.

'It doesn't matter,' she said. 'It doesn't matter.' She had her ear cocked on one side, listening to that piano-player.

'I like you,' I said. 'You're kind to me. You speak to me nicely.'

'I like you, too, Joey,' she said. 'You're a nice guy. What a pity some woman won't look after you, say nice things to you all the time.'

I scowled. 'I don't like dames,' I said. 'Dames are

not good for me. Nick told me. He knows. He knows everything.'

Her head was cocked to one side, like she wanted to catch every note coming out from that silver-tongued piano. 'If Nick said that, he knows what he's talking about, I guess,' she said.

'Nick knows everything,' I told her. 'He's a fine guy. You oughta talk to Nick. It'd make you feel good, too.'

She looked at me, and her eyes were sparkling excitedly. 'D'you think I could see him, Joey? Just for a few moments? I'd like to thank him for everything. Can you do it, Joey? Can you?'

She was so eager, I'd have promised anything to keep that happy sparkle in her eyes. 'Sure,' I said. 'I'll get Nick. I'll bring him down to see you. I'll bring him tomorrow.'

She sighed deliciously. 'If only you could. Just for a few foments.' Her eyes were kinda dreamy now. 'He's such a wonderful guy,' she said.

She was right there. Nick was a wonderful guy. 'I'll do it,' I boasted. 'I'll bring him tomorrow.'

The music changed tempo, became slow and passionate, throbbing wildly on the low notes. Her head was cocked on one side again. 'Who's that playing, Joey?'

'It's a new guy,' I said. 'He only started yesterday. Practising up some of the numbers, I guess.'

She looked along the corridor towards the nightclub, kinda hesitated. Then, she looked at me. 'Could we ... that is ... Could we go and listen?'

'Sure,' I said. 'Anything you want. Will you do it again? Just once more?' I pleaded.

'Okay, *Joey*,' she said. 'You're a nice guy, *Joey*.' I

warmed all over, happy and contented inside, just the way it I was when Nick spoke to me. 'Straight along the corridor,' I said. 'It'll be all right. I can take you in there. But say it just once more, will you? Just once more.'

The nightclub was in darkness except for the solitary dimmed light over the piano. It was almost ghostlike in that large room now it was empty, the chairs standing on the tables enveloped in shadow while the soft silvery notes rang around the silent walls and furniture.

The guy was working at it, crouched over the keyboard, eyes half-closed and his body moving as though he was draining his body and mind of strength so he could funnel it through to his fingers.

We crossed over to him, on tiptoe. He sensed we were there, but didn't look up, went on playing with the same intensity of feeling. We edged right up alongside him, leaned our elbows on the piano. There was a kinda dreamy, enraptured look in Sheila's eyes. She stayed that way all the time he was playing, right up until the last notes sounded, hovered on the air and then died away.

The young guy looked up. He was a nice young guy, with long wavy hair that brushed back over his head, soft brown eyes and a little wisp of a moustache.

Sheila said: 'Don't stop. Please play some more.'

His eyes twinkled when he laughed. 'Am I keeping you folks awake?'

'Please,' pleaded Sheila. 'You play beautifully. Do go on playing.'

He looked down at the keyboard, ran his fingers up and down the white notes, and a cascading, silvery stream poured out and splashed over us. 'What d'you want me to play?'

'Do you know *Moonlight*?' she asked.

'Which one? This one?' The silvery cascade turned into a soft, haunting harmony. The music kinda did things to me, soothed me, made me wanna close my eyes and dream.

'That's it,' Sheila whispered. She half-closed her eyes, put her head on one side, listened intently, swaying gently with the rhythm. When he reached the refrain, she began to hum, softly at first, then more loudly and more richly as he went on. When he got to the end, he said: 'Sounds like you know music. Do you sing at all?'

'Just to myself,' she chuckled.

'Try it again. Sing it this time.'

She laughed away his suggestion. 'I couldn't. I couldn't, really.'

'Sure you can,' he encouraged. 'You've got the feeling for it. I can tell that.'

'But I couldn't ...' she began to protest.

'Sure you can, Sheila,' I said. 'You can sing. You can sing good.'

She looked at me, she looked at the young guy. 'Okay, then,' she said. 'We'll try it.'

She could sing! The way she sang made me want to close my eyes and dream and never wake up. The young guy was crazy about her voice. He played piece after piece, making her sing all of them. Finally, he got her singing the words from the music. It musta gone on for a coupla hours or maybe more. Yet at the end of that time, it seemed like we'd been there only a few minutes.

The young fella said: 'I mustn't keep you out of bed any longer. But we'll try this again. Tomorrow night, huh?'

'I'd love to,' she said. There was an eager sparkle in her eyes.

'What's your name?' he asked.

'Sheila,' she told him. 'I'm the ...' She hesitated, shot me a shy glance, and then: 'I work here.'

'Call me Henry,' he said. He chuckled. 'Once in a while, I get called other names. But I'm hoping you won't have occasion to use those.'

'Are you here every night?'

'You bet,' he said enthusiastically. 'And don't you forget tomorrow.'

It was that way every night. The young guy playing and her singing, like it was only when his fingers touched the notes that she began to live. They didn't seem to mind me being there, but I got a queer kinda feeling, like they was living in a world of their own and I was living on a separate planet. They gave each other meaningful looks, said things that didn't make sense to me but caused them to laugh together, shared some kind of emotion together that was a secret between them that no-one else knew anything about.

Maybe I am slow about some things. Maybe I do get hazy at times, not very clear about what's happening or what's going to happen. But I'm different to other people. I know it. I know things other people don't. It's a feeling inside me I get. I know things I just can't explain, as though some part of my mind reaches out, gets a grip on understanding. Like the time Nick had Orelli working for him. Everyone liked Orelli. Nick liked him too, helped him make money. I knew something then. I warned Nick, but he wouldn't listen. That Orelli was jealous of Nick, wanted to harm him some way. Every time I got near the guy and heard him talking, I knew what was in his mind. It was something I knew that nobody else knew. There's something special about me, the same way the haziness is something special about me.

That night when Orelli opened up Nick's safe and shot the head waiter when he was interrupted, I reminded Nick, told him I'd warned him.

Nick wasn't pleased with me that night. He told me to shut up, told me I was shooting off my mouth. But maybe Nick was mad because he realised I'd been right all along. Maybe he realised if he'd listened to me, he wouldn't have had the bother of sending after Orelli. And afterwards he was never really happy about Orelli, because although they caught up with him, by that time there was only a little dough left. Orelli hadn't even hidden it away. He'd spent it. He kept swearing he'd spent it right up until the last minute. I guess he must have spent it at that. No guy who's hidden dough would have held out the way Orelli did. No dough is worth what he went through.

In the same way I knew about Orelli, I knew about Sheila and Henry. There was something special between them. It was so strong, it began to make me feel bad. I felt in the way, wasn't wanted.

Then one night after the singing, Sheila had to go back to the ladies' powder room for a magazine she'd left behind.

'What d'ya want that for?' I asked, as I accompanied her upstairs to her room.

Her cheeks were flushed and her eyes were sparkling like singing was champagne to her. 'I like looking at the pictures, Joey,' she explained.

'What pictures?'

'Dresses and things. Pictures of grand ladies, wearing expensive clothes. Like this one.'

She showed me a picture of a dress. I didn't see how anyone could get worked up about a piece of coloured material. But it kinda intoxicated her so she pored over the picture wistfully, sighed like it would be heaven if she had a dress like that.

I sneaked into her room the next morning, found the magazine, tore out the picture. The firm advertising it was located in the classy district. It got me all hot and bothered going there, and I couldn't get what I wanted because they asked for measurements.

For a time, that got me stymied. Then I had an idea, slipped into Sheila's room one evening, borrowed her spare dress and took that down to the dress shop.

A week later, it was ready. I gave it to Sheila the same night when she came off duty.

'Oh, thank you, Joey,' she said. 'But what is it?'

'Something you wanted,' I said.

She was anxious to get to the piano and start singing. 'Thank you so much, Joey,' she said. But she didn't seem very interested in it. 'I'll look at it later.'

'Look at it now, please,' I said. 'Do look at it now.'

'All right, Joey.'

She may have been disinterested before she opened the packet, but once she got the wrapping off, lifted the lid and saw it, her eyes widened and her fingers trembled as she pulled it out and stared at it with a kinda wondrous delight in her eyes, before she timidly held it up against herself.

'Joey!' she whispered. 'It's wonderful! It's wonderful!'

'Say it,' I pleaded. 'Say it again.'

'Oh, Joey,' she said. 'You're such a dear person. Sometimes I could almost love you, even though …' She broke off, blushed, added quickly: 'I must try it on.'

I didn't understand her. It was just a silly old dress, just a bit of material. It cost a helluva lotta dough, too. They called it a *Single Model Evening Gown*. That didn't mean anything special to me. It did to them though. They charged more for that dress than it cost me for a complete winter rig-out.

I guess it was worth it, giving her all that pleasure. When she came out of the powder room, she looked like a queen, her bare shoulders gleaming, the white bodice of the gown drawn in tightly around her narrow waist, then billowing out like a cloud. She walked up and down the corridor displaying it, twirled, watched the way it billowed around her legs, and was radiant with happiness.

It didn't seem to me anything to make a fuss about. Except I liked the sound of it. It kinda whispered when she walked. It made a nice noise. I kept listening to it, listening to the sound of it, not wanting it to stop.

'It's wonderful, Joey!' she breathed. 'You're so wonderful to me. I don't know how I can ever thank you.' Her eyes were dancing. 'I must show Henry. He'll love it.'

Maybe he did, or maybe he was just pretending. I wouldn't know. He certainly sounded enthusiastic. And then when he started playing, and she leaned up against the piano and sang in her low, husky voice, I knew she ought to be on the stage, ought to have one of those big white lights gleaming on her. For the first time, I felt really pleased about that dress, felt proud it was me who'd bought it for her, and proud Henry said she was beautiful with that breathless note in his voice.

I'd forgotten about asking Big Nick to come; so him coming into the nightclub that night of all nights, when she was wearing that dress and singing so hauntingly, was coincidence.

I didn't see him at first. Neither did the other two. He stood in the shadows, the red eye of his cigarette gleaming and reflecting against his stiff, white shirt-front. He waited until they'd reached the end of a number, then walked over to us, with lazy, languorous strides. The soft rap of his shoes drew our attention and then we were all watching him, feeling guilty and wondering if he'd be mad.

He came right up to us, stared at Sheila so long that she dropped her eyes. Then he looked at Henry.

'Why are you still here?' he demanded.

Henry flushed, half-climbed to his feet. 'Getting in a little practice, sir,' he said. 'I hoped you wouldn't mind.'

'Nope,' said Nick. 'It was fine.' He jerked with his head. 'You can go now.'

Henry hesitated. He looked at Sheila. She was standing with head bowed, demurely looking at the floor.

'I said you can go!' rasped Nick, and there was no disobeying him.

Nick lit a cigarette, waited until Henry had left, before he said in the soft voice he often used with dames: 'Where did you spring from, honey?'

She looked up at him then, nervously, apprehensively. 'I – er – I – er – work here,' she got out.

'Well!' he said with satisfaction. 'Why didn't somebody tell me?' He stepped back a coupla paces, looked her over slowly and deliberately. 'A swell dish like you working for me, and I didn't know it! Who's been keeping me in the dark?'

'It's the dame, boss,' I said. 'You remember? You said I could give her a job.'

He obviously didn't remember. He said vaguely: 'That's right. Told you to give her a job, didn't I?'

'It was kind of you, mister,' she said. She dropped

her eyes again, like Nick was too important a guy to talk to face to face.

'You've got a cute voice, kid,' he said. He put his forefinger under her chin, lifted her head so her wide, clear eyes stared straight into his. 'Just what do I employ you to do, anyway?'

She went red. Red as a beetroot. 'It's a small job,' she faltered, in a weak voice. Then she added eagerly: 'But I'm very pleased to have it.'

He grinned. 'You're kidding me, aren't you, honey? You don't work here. I'd have seen you around if you worked here.'

'Not where she works,' I broke in cheerfully and loudly.

He ignored me. 'What do you do, honey?'

'The powder room,' she whispered. 'The ladies' powder room.'

It jolted him. 'The powder room!' he exploded.

'She wanted the job, boss,' I interrupted. 'She didn't mind what it was.'

'Powder room!' he echoed again. 'That's crazy! A swell dish like you piloting the chain-pullers! Who thought up that crazy, idea?'

'It was Sinclaire,' I said. 'The only job he had was …'

'A crazy idea giving her a job like that,' he muttered. He was looking her over again, like a collector examining a curio piece. 'Got a voice, got a good figure,' he said, like he was talking to himself. 'Not exactly beautiful, but she's got that innocent kinda expression that goes down. A few bucks spent at the hairdresser's would help a lot.' He frowned. 'Who thought up the crazy idea of giving her that job?'

'Please, Mr Fenner,' she said quickly. 'I'm happy,

really I am. You've been so kind to me, so good. I'm very happy with my work. I don't want you to think I'm discontented …'

She had big brown eyes. They were full of devotion, like a spaniel's. Big Nick did something to her. I felt that if he pushed her over, wiped his feet on her, she'd be the happiest dame alive.

'With that voice of yours,' he said thoughtfully, 'you oughta be under the spotlight. You oughta be earning money, real money. Not peanuts!'

The germ of suspicion started working in his mind. He gave Sheila the once-over again. It seemed Big Nick knew about dresses the same as he knew about everything else. 'Wait a minute,' he said ominously. 'That dress cost dough. Where d'ya get enough dough to buy that kinda dress?'

She was awe-stricken by him, scared speechless. Her eyes unwillingly flicked to me, switched back to him.

Nick turned to me slowly. His eyes were like gimlets boring into my brain. 'Did you buy this dress, Joey?'

'Sure, Nick,' I said. 'The little dame wanted it. I got it for her.'

He stood staring at me, breathing deeply, almost like he was counting. Then he turned back to the dame, and this time his voice was harsh.

'You been making a monkey out of this sap?' he asked. 'You been playing him for a sucker?'

Her eyes were frantic now. 'No, no. Please don't think that. He's so good and kind. It was his idea. He did it all by himself. I didn't know anything about it and …'

'Did she ask you for a dress, Joey?' he rasped loudly.

'Gee, boss,' I said indignantly. 'She didn't ask me for nothing. It was my idea. I thought it up.'

He calmed down, said softly: 'It's okay, honey. Just for a moment I thought you might be ...'

'But I wouldn't,' she said. 'I wouldn't dream of ...'

'No, I guess not.' He looked her over again, a greedy kinda look. She didn't see the expression in his eyes, because her own eyes were once more lowered demurely.

'I'll think about you, kid,' he said. 'You oughta do better than waiting for folks while they're swinging on a chain. Just stick around. I'll think of something for you.'

He didn't say goodnight. He sauntered away like a god who in his own good time is gonna perform a miracle, transform her world and her life so she herself would become almost godlike.

'He's so handsome, isn't he, Joey?' she said when he had gone.

'One of the best guys,' I told her. 'Without Nick I'd ...'

'A real gentleman,' she whispered excitedly. 'And speaking to me like I was someone of his own class. He's so masterful, too, so proud, so strong.' Her eyes were wide and swimmy when she looked up at me. 'You couldn't help loving a guy like that, could you, Joey? You just couldn't help it, could you?'

'Nick's been a good guy to me,' I said. 'I don't know what I'd have done without Nick. He means everything.'

'I can understand that,' she said softly. 'I know just how you feel.'

9

A few days later, Nick said I had to drive Lola into town. I hated those trips. Lola always looked at me with those ice-cold, contemptuous eyes of hers, instructed me to wait, kept me waiting hours while she visited a beauty salon or a dress designer. And she complained to Nick if I wandered away to look at the shop windows and wasn't waiting for her in the car when she got back.

But Nick wanted me to drive her, and he was such a good guy I'd do anything for him. As it happened, it was a good job I was with Lola. I was able to tell Nick exactly what happened.

It was a hairdresser she visited. I waited outside for maybe a coupla hours before she finally clip-clopped through the door with a smiling, wavy-haired, womanish-looking guy bowing her out like she'd spent a fortune. Maybe she had, at that.

I opened the door of the car, held it that way while she climbed in. A couple of those Feds drifted along out of nowhere. 'Keep holding the door that way,' said one Fed, the one called Jake.

Nick had told me we weren't ever to make trouble with Feds. Not ever. I did what the guy told me, held the door open so he and the other Fed could climb in alongside Lola.

She let out a squawk that sounded like she was being kidnapped. The squawk cut short when they flashed their badges. 'Tell the trained monkey to climb in front and keep quiet,' said Jake.

Lola glared at him venomously, gulped, said to me: 'You heard him, Joey. Climb in up front and keep your ears flapping.' We sat there in the car with all the windows shut while ordinary folks were passing up and down outside on their private business.

Jake said: 'We've been waiting around a long while for a chance to talk with you.'

Lola said: 'I'm saying nothing until I see my mouthpiece.'

'You don't need a mouthpiece, lady,' said Jake. 'We're not charging you with anything. We're just asking questions. You're kick's special, aren't you? Live over the nightclub with him?'

She bristled. 'What's it to you, flatfoot? It's my life, ain't it? It's my business how I choose to live.'

'Sure,' he said. His eyes narrowed. 'But a smart dame like you knows the kinda company she keeps. Big Nick's in trouble, real trouble. That means it's likely you'll be in trouble too.'

She stared at him. There was concern in those blue eyes. She asked suspiciously: 'What kinda trouble?'

'Murder,' said the other Fed.

'You're crazy,' Lola said doubtfully. 'You don't know what you're talking about.' But she was just a little scared.

'Nick killed that cop,' said Jake.

'You're crazy,' she repeated. 'Nick wouldn't kill a cop. He's too smart for that.' Then, as though she'd suddenly realised that despite herself she was talking, she added: 'Aw, leave me alone, will ya? You make me sick. Scram, will ya?'

'That's okay, lady. We're going. But just one word of warning. You're in with high-stepping company. You've gotta step high yourself. You've gotta be smart, too. Those who fly highest, fall hardest. When Nick falls, he's gonna come down hard, and he's gonna pull down everything else with him. So I'm warning you, lady. You've got just one chance. Any time you wanna talk, you know where to find us, and we're always ready to listen. Maybe a little talking at the right time will save your neck when the crash comes.'

'You're crazy,' she said. 'You don't know what you're talking about. You don't know a thing.'

'Think it over,' said Jake. 'That's all I'm warning you, lady. Just think it over.'

They climbed out of the car then, slammed the door, leaving Lola sitting bolt upright, angry and ruffled like a hen that's scampered across the road in front of a speeding car. 'What the hell!' she flared at me. 'Damned cops talking to me that way! Trying to hang something on *me*!'

'Tell Nick,' I suggested. 'He'll know what to do.'

'Sure I'll tell him!' she flared. 'Nick will crucify them.'

Lola seemed kinda scared, wanted me to be with her when she told Nick about it later.

'That's everything that happened, Nick,' she said. 'Ask Joey. He was there. He heard every word.' She was afraid Nick might think she'd talked too much.

Nick scowled. 'Why d'you let them guys talk to you that way?' he demanded angrily. 'You shoulda ordered them out. They've got nothing on you.'

She looked at him anxiously. 'What did they mean, Nick? What did they mean about murder?, You didn't kill that cop, did you?'

He stared at her steadily, narrowed his eyes. 'You ain't getting ideas?' he demanded.

'Why no, Nick,' she said quickly, just a little too quickly. 'I wouldn't think anything like that.' Her voice rose a little, got a little desperate. 'There's nothing for me to know, is there, Nick? That was just their bluff, wasn't it?' She became almost desperate, trying to convince him. 'Even if I did know anything, Nick, I wouldn't say a word, Nick. You know that. I wouldn't say a word.'

He didn't say anything. He just stared at her steadily. The expression in his eyes frightened her. She backed away from him, scared. 'You know me, Nick. You don't think I'd say anything? You mustn't believe that!'

'Get out!' he snarled. 'Get out! Lose yourself for a coupla hours.'

Nick gave me a job to do. 'Clear all these wardrobes out,' he ordered. 'I want this room cleaned up and everything of Lola's packed in cases. Don't waste time on it, get cracking!'

I liked doing that work. Lola's clothes were so soft to touch. There were dozens of dresses, all different materials, all different colours, and all of them feeling so soft and smooth. They felt like Big Nick's voice, soft, silky and comforting like black velvet. There were lots of other clothes too. Fragile, delicate underclothes that whispered in my fingers, so fine I could crush them in one hand, hold them without it showing they were in my hand.

I'd almost finished when Lola came back. She stood poised in the doorway, glaring around as though she couldn't believe her eyes. Then her eyes flamed, blue eyes burning with searing anger. 'What the hell are you doing?' she stormed.

I was holding a sky-blue dress that was as light as a feather, soft like smooth skin. Lola got me worried. I dropped the dress on top of the others, thrust it hastily down in the case.

That little action seemed to drive Lola mad. She had a big mouth. She opened it wide, screeched in fury, dropped everything she was carrying and sprang at me with outspread fingers tipped with blood-red, slashing nails.

Nick repeatedly told me I wasn't to get into fights. I dodged away from her, dodged around the settee. She came after me, screeching furiously, crazy enough to shred my face with those long nails, picking up anything she could lay her hands on and throwing it with savage force.

Maybe she'd have caught me if it had gone on long enough. But it was Nick again. He was always helping me, getting me out of trouble and making me feel good.

He came through from his own bedroom, which was right next to Lola's room. 'Cut it out, Lola!' he roared.

His voice brought her to a stop. But it didn't cool her anger. 'Look what that crazy dope's been doing to my clothes,' she shrilled. 'Just look at what he's done ...'

'He was doing what I told him,' rasped Nick.

She gaped. 'You told him to!'

'That's right,' said Nick. His eyes were narrowed and he kinda squared his shoulders like he was ready for trouble.

'Are you out of your mind?' she demanded.

'No,' he said softly. 'Just being smart. You're a

know-nothing dame and you're gonna stop that way. You give me a pain in the neck. You're all washed up, understand? You're out! You're out on your ear. Understand?'

She understood. But she didn't believe it. She tried to laugh it off. 'You don't know what you're saying, Nick. You're crazy to talk that way.'

'Think so?' He put his hand in his inside pocket, pulled out a wallet and peeled off century notes from the thick wad he always carried. I thought he'd never stop counting. Finally he did, rolled the money in a ball, threw it towards Lola. 'That'll keep you until you get another sucker to pay your expenses,' he said. 'Your bags can be sent on. Now get out, will ya? Get out quick! It gives me the creeps seeing you around.'

He'd convinced her now. She ran over to him, grabbed him by the coat lapels, desperately tried to shake understanding into him. 'I don't know what you're thinking, Nick. But it's all wrong. If I knew anything, I wouldn't squeal to the cops. I wanna stop with you, Nick. I've been good to you. You can't just turn me out this way.'

'Have I gotta knock it into your head with a sledge-hammer?' he demanded brutally. 'You're all washed up. You're finished. Understand?' He emphasised the last question by thrusting her away from him so she fell sideways, sprawled on the carpet with a thump.

She was crying now. 'Nick,' she pleaded. 'Don't do it! For God's sake, don't do it! I wouldn't squeal ...'

Nick was perfectly at ease. He lifted his left arm elegantly, consulted his wrist watch. 'You've thirty seconds to scram,' he said coolly. 'Thirty seconds to snatch the dough and scram. That's if you're sensible.

Otherwise Maxie and Whitey will persuade you.'

She believed him now right enough. Her tearful eyes stared up at him piteously. And Nick was really acting now. You'd have thought he was a real hard guy the way he intoned softly: *'Ten seconds – fifteen seconds – twenty seconds...'*

She'd been with Nick long enough to know he meant what he said. At twenty seconds, she was on her feet. At twenty-five seconds, she'd gathered up the loose dough he'd flung on the floor, and at thirty seconds, with a look of hate written on her face, she was out of the door, slamming it behind her.

Nick frowned at the closed door for several seconds. Then he looked at me, and a broad grin spread across his face. He shrugged his shoulders like he'd just got rid of a dead weight. 'That's settled that little trouble. Now get busy, will ya, Joey? Get the cleaners up here. Get this room cleaned up, get rid of all those bits of lipstick, curlers, cotton wool and stuff. Get the whole lot cleaned out, huh?'

'Sure, Nick,' I said, grinning happily, happy because Nick was happy.

'I want new sheets on the bed, too,' he said. 'The best sheets you can get. You go buy them yourself, Joey. The finest silken sheets, hand-made and hand-embroidered. Can you do it, Joey?'

'Sure, boss,' I said, delighted that he'd given me a special job to do for him.

'That's the idea, Joey,' he said. 'You do it for Nick, huh?'

'Sure, boss,' I grinned. 'I'll do it just the way you want.'

It was three days later when Nick told me the good news.

'Joey,' he said. 'You like that little dame? The one that sings?'

'Sure, boss,' I said. 'She talks good to me. She says nice things.'

'That's fine, Joey,' he said. 'That's real fine. How would you like she has a better room, one that's more comfortable? All the dresses she wants, too?'

'Gee, boss,' I said eagerly. 'She'd like that fine. I'd like it for her.'

'I tell you what you do, Joey,' he said. 'Go get that dame. Bring her up here.'

She was awed, almost scared. I brought her up to Nick's apartment, and she sat on the edge of a chair, like she considered herself unworthy to sit on it properly.

Nick seated himself opposite her, nonchalantly, puffing a cigarette. 'I'm gonna give you a break, kid,' he said. 'I'm gonna give you a better job.'

Her eyes widened with delight. 'That's so kind of you, Mr Fenner. I must admit I've been very happy here, and I've nothing to complain about …'

'I'm gonna make you a singer,' he said. 'You can do a coupla numbers every evening.'

Her eyes widened even more. 'But, Mr Fenner, I've never sung to people before and …'

He hushed her with masterful hand motions. 'You haven't a thing to worry about, kid,' he said. 'You don't sing until you really want to. If you're not in the mood, well you don't do it.' He rushed on swiftly. 'You'll get a hundred bucks a week, board and lodging. Does that suit you?'

It was too good to be true. She just couldn't believe it. She gasped, tried to find words.

'I don't want an argument about it,' said Nick abruptly. 'Answer yes or no. Is it a deal? Yes or no?'

'I ... yes.'

'Good, that's settled then.' He said it with the air of a man who's completed a boring preliminary. He got to his feet, jerked his head at Sheila for her to follow him. 'Come along, kid. I'll show you your new quarters.'

She was happy, excited, hardly able to believe her good fortune. But I noticed a change in her, as we passed from the lounge into his bedroom, through the communicating door into the bedroom that Lola used to occupy. Sheila's steps grew slower and slower, timid, almost reluctant.

Nick sure had fitted up that bedroom swell. It'd been cleaned up real good, draped with brightly-coloured chintz curtains and drapes, spruced up like a college girl going to her first dance.

'Like it, kid?' asked Nick. He was grinning happily like Father Christmas dishing out toys to the Dead End Kids.

She looked bewildered, a little afraid. She said, 'Yes, but ...'

Nick was excited like a boy, showing her everything. He interrupted. 'These buttons on the bed. You've got the names underneath. This one for drinks, this one for the chambermaid, this one for a messenger. Get the idea, honey?' He rushed on, talking volubly. 'You've got your own radio and television built into the wall there. Press this button, see? The doors slide back and you can sit up in bed and watch the television in comfort.'

He crossed the room to the built-in wardrobe, slid back the wide doors, displayed a rack of beautiful dresses. He indicated them with a proud gesture. 'All your size, honey,' he said. 'Everything you want, from a morning dress to an evening gown. How'd you like it? Nice, huh?'

I didn't understand Sheila. She'd been pleased enough when I gave her that dress. Now she was getting a whole cupboardful, she looked apprehensive, kinda scared. 'Mr Fenner,' she said. 'I couldn't. You surely understand that. I couldn't accept ...'

He waved down her objections. 'Quit worrying about it, honey,' he said. 'I've got plenty of dough.' He gestured to the dresses. 'Them's peanuts. Have more any time you want. Have anything you want.'

'Please listen to me, Mr Fenner,' she interrupted. 'There's something you should ...'

Nick had reached into the wardrobe, fished out a sky-blue dress that sounded like music as it swayed on its hanger. 'Put this on, honey,' he said. 'That black dress gives me the creeps. Put this on. Let's see how it fits.'

He thrust the dress into her hand and she stared at it, dominated by Nick. 'G'wan,' he encouraged. 'Put it on. It won't take a minute.'

She looked at the dress longingly. She was dying to try it on. She looked at Nick. Then she looked at me. She moistened her lips. 'I'd like to try it on, Mr Fenner,' she said. 'But ...' She looked at me and looked at him again, meaningfully.

'That's okay, honey,' said Nick, with another airy wave of his hands. 'You don't have to worry about Joey. He don't know what time it is. D'you get what I mean?' He winked at her.

She looked at me. She looked at him. She looked at the dress. She said, in a slightly worried voice: 'You don't mean I should change with you both here?'

He looked at her suspiciously. 'You kidding,

honey?'

Her eyes were frank and innocent, her face questioning: 'Kidding?'

A suggestion of harshness entered his voice. 'Aw, honey. Don't waste time. Don't be childish. You ain't got a thing to worry about.'

'Well ...' she said, doubtfully. She stared at him, weighing him up. Then, as though making a sudden resolution, she turned away from us, loosened buttons, bent, took the hem of her tawdry black frock between her fingers and straightened up, drawing it over her head.

Underneath, she was wearing a frayed slip. Like they were drawn by a magnet, Nick's eyes went to the smooth skin of her thighs, which showed above the tops of her black stockings. 'I've bought underclothes for you as well, honey,' he said hoarsely. 'Everything you want. Lots of black lace and transparent georgette. Nice, huh?'

She was acutely self-conscious, struggled into the dress quickly, pulled it straight, turned around to face us with flushed cheeks.

Nick surveyed her critically, nodded his head with satisfaction. 'You look swell, kid,' he said. 'Really lovely. With a hair-do, high-heeled shoes, some make-up and a manicure, you'd pass for a film star.'

Yeah, he was right. Just changing her dress did make her look different. I could see how, after going to a hairdresser, she wouldn't look mousy and insignificant any longer. She'd look pretty, real pretty.

'That dress is fine, honey,' said Nick. 'Now let's see how you look in those undies.'

I didn't think anyone's face could go so red. It was as though she'd been fighting a battle inside herself all the time and now had found the strength to make a stand. She threw back her head, squared her shoulders. 'Mr Fenner,' she said firmly but clearly. 'I think you oughta understand. I want to work. But I don't want to …' She broke off.

His eyes narrowed. 'Meaning what?'

She gestured around the room, towards the wardrobe, the bed and Nick's bedroom next door. 'You don't understand, Mr Fenner. That isn't the sort of thing I do. I'm not that kind.' There were tears in her eyes now. 'It's not that I'm ungrateful. But I'm not … that way. I just couldn't do it.'

Nick stared at her. The way his brow puckered showed he was having difficulty in understanding her. There was a note of incredulity in his voice. 'Whad'ya trying to say, honey? Put it on the line. Don't speak in riddles.'

She took a deep breath. Her cheeks were flaming. 'Mr Fenner,' she said clearly, 'I don't want to feel that anybody's buying me. I'd like to sing in your club. I'd like a better job. But …' Once again she looked towards his bedroom. 'I couldn't do it, Mr Fenner. I'm just not … that kind.'

Nick stared at her so long I was afraid he'd gone dumb. It was like a battle was going on inside him, too, fear and rage, fighting with the ache to obtain possession of something. Finally he said slowly, with a kinda fake note in his voice: 'I oughta be annoyed with you, kid. You got me wrong right from the start. You oughta think before you assume things.'

Her eyes widened.

Nick dug down in his pocket, pulled out a Yale key, tossed it across the room so it fell on the bed. He thumbed towards his bedroom door. 'Better close that door,' he told her. 'You keep that locked day and night.

Understand?' He pointed towards another door. 'That door leads into the corridor. That's your own door. You go in and out as you want without interference.' He pointed towards the wardrobe. 'A singer in my nightclub has got to look right. She's got to have the clothes to go with the job. Call them stage props if you like.' He took a deep breath, stared at her until she dropped her eyes. 'Maybe my intentions could have been misunderstood. But you can get those kinda ideas out of your head right now, lady.'

The flush had drained from her cheeks so now she was pale. All the fight had gone out of her. She was pathetic and penitent. 'I'm so sorry, Mr Fenner,' she stammered. 'I didn't realise ... I thought ... I never meant ...'

'Okay,' he growled. 'Skip it. You've got a phone. Fix up for the hairdresser to work on those rats' tails. This is your room from now on. Somebody will bring your other things over later.' He jerked his head at me. 'Come along, Joey,' he said, as though I was the only friend he could rely on. Then, as we reached the door of his bedroom, he said over his shoulder, with a kinda bitterness: 'Don't forget to lock the door after me.'

Nick was in a temper. Even though his face was calm and his voice smooth, he was flaming inside. I could sense it, the way I can sense these things. We went through to his lounge, where he got out a bottle of whisky, poured himself a generous dose. He drained it in one gulp. Then he looked at me steadily. 'What d'ya make of that, Joey?' he demanded. 'A dame that acts sweet and innocent – and really is!'

'She's pretty,' I said stoutly. 'She's got a nice voice. She makes me feel good.'

Nick scowled. 'She makes me feel good, too.' He

poured more whisky. 'Too good!' He sighed. 'You wouldn't understand, though.'

'She likes singing,' I told him. 'She sings real good.'

He held his glass up to the light, examined it carefully. But his mind was far away. 'Remember one thing, Joey,' he said. 'If you want a thing and you can't get it one way, there's always a dozen other ways.'

'Yes, boss,' I agreed enthusiastically. I hadn't the faintest idea what he was talking about.

'She likes you, doesn't she, Joey?'

'I like her too. I like her voice.'

'Teach her to play gin rummy, Joey,' he said. 'You like playing that, don't you, Joey?'

I nodded my head eagerly.

'That's right,' Nick grinned. 'We'll play gin rummy every night. Yeah, in my lounge. Go tell her about it.'

'Sure, Nick,' I said. 'I'll like that fine.'

I'm supposed to be slow, not understand things quickly like other folks. I guess it's true about some things. But with other things, I'm quicker than anyone else. About people I like, for example.

I noticed things about Nick no-one else noticed. I saw the change that took place in him during the next few days. He did things that wasn't like him. Playing gin rummy, for example. Most nights Nick was out, attending to business, or visiting the cat house, or on private business he didn't tell me about.

But during the next few days, he changed completely, sat up after the nightclub had closed, playing gin rummy with me and Sheila. And he played for peanuts too; not the big money he usually played for.

Nick's character had changed too. He became

quiet, wasn't so masterful, didn't talk so much, and most of the time was watching Sheila intently and admiringly, doing little things for her, like getting a chair, opening a door, and talking to her real nice. Things he'd never done for any other dame.

I noticed Sheila too. It was like she was softening up. She kept watching Nick with a kinda soft light in her eyes that was almost worship mingled with adoration.

When we'd been playing gin rummy for almost a week and had finished the last game for the evening, Nick said quietly: 'You still don't trust me, do you?'

'Oh, but I do, Nick,' she protested. 'I think you're one of the swellest guys ...'

'You don't trust me,' he insisted.

Her eyes were hurt. She raised one eyebrow slightly more than the other. 'Why do you say that, Nick?'

'You hurt me,' he said sincerely. 'Every night you rub it in. Every night I hear that damned key turn in the lock.'

There was a strange expression in her eyes as she stared at him. 'Do I really hurt you that bad, Nick?'

'You don't trust me,' he said sullenly.

Later, when she went to bed, behind her back Nick motioned to me to keep quiet. Sheila said goodnight, passed through Nick's bedroom into her own bedroom. Nick was tensed and listening when she closed the door. I listened, too. It didn't happen tonight. She didn't turn the key in the lock. Nick heaved a sigh. Then he nodded towards his cocktail cabinet. 'Give me a scotch, Joey. A large scotch.'

I sat there with him, watched as he drank, and tried to understand what was going on in his mind. He was sunk into himself, thinking deeply like he was figuring angles. Suddenly he got up, went through to his bedroom. A little later, he came out wearing his dressing-gown. 'Stick around, Joey,' he ordered. 'I may want you.'

'Sure, boss,' I said.

'I might have a little trouble,' he told me. 'I may want your help keeping that dame quiet. Understand?'

'Sure, Nick,' I said. I looked at him obediently, wondering what he had in mind.

He looked at me, shook his head sorrowfully. 'Poor Joey,' he said. 'You don't understand it, fella. Do you?'

I dropped my eyes, felt humble. 'No, boss,' I admitted.

'Just stick around anyway,' he told me.

He went through to his bedroom, started pussy-footing around. That got me curious. I just had to know what he was up to. I tiptoed across to his bedroom, peered inside. He wasn't there. But the door at the far end which led into Sheila's bedroom was standing partly open.

I've often wondered why Nick and other guys spent so much time locked up with dames in rooms at the cat house. This was my chance to find out.

But I was scared. Nick might be mad at me. I waited all of five minutes before I had the courage to tiptoe across to Sheila's door and watch through the crack of the door jamb.

Sheila was fast asleep, breathing softly, one white arm out-flung across the pillows. There was a sweet, innocent look on her face. She looked so good, so childlike, she reminded me of the pictures they used to have in the Bible they tried to teach me to read at school.

It was strange the way Nick was standing there, staring down at her. He was frozen, frightened to move in case he disturbed her. There was something good about the expression on his face, too. Nick always looked handsome. But I'd never seen his face look quite this way before. It was sad, almost … – yeah, the guys would rib me about this word – … almost holy!

I stood watching him through the crack in the door until my bones ached. Then he moved. Slowly he bent over her, pressed his lips to her forehead. He did it so gently, she didn't even stir. Then he straightened up quickly, turned away and began to tiptoe out of the room.

I was smart enough to be back in the lounge before he got there. He hadn't got that holy look any more. He was scowling.

'Okay, Joey,' he gritted. 'You can go now.'

None of this made sense to me. I didn't understand what kick guys got out of being in a room alone with a dame if that's what they did.

I got to the door, half-turned with my hand on the handle. 'Can I have a drink before I go to bed, boss?'

'No, Joey,' he said gently. 'You lay off drink. And remember what I tell ya. Lay off dames too. Understand?'

I turned away, closed the door quietly after me.

10

Big Nick *had* changed. At last even the other guys noticed it. As the weeks went past, Maxie and Whitey talked between themselves.

'That pansy, innocent-looking Judy did it,' complained Maxie. 'She's so good, she scares the pants off me. I'm scared she'll get the boss that way. Make him soft and goody-goody, maybe Bible-punching.'

Whitey said with a scowl: 'She's playing him like a fish. He hasn't made first base with her yet. Just a goodnight kiss. That's all.' He gave a harsh chuckle that didn't show humour. 'Can you believe that? A guy with Nick's experience falling for a dame who thinks it a crime when a guy mentions the word 'legs'!'

It got me mad them talking that way about the boss. I said fiercely: 'Nick knows what he's doing. He's clever. He knows more than anybody.'

Whitey growled. 'Shut your mouth, you dumb-bell!' he rasped. 'Why, you ...'

Maxie interrupted him fiercely. 'Cut it out, will ya, Whitey? You'll overdo it one day. Cut it out, will ya? For Chrissakes, cut it out!'

The hammering was in my head. It was starting again.

Maxie said softly, soothingly: 'Take it easy, Joey. Take it easy now, boy.'

The words were something to hold on to. I reached out, held them tightly. I fell the hammering slowly die away, and found I could breathe easily.

'You can overdo it,' Maxie told Whitey grimly.

'Aw!' said Whitey. But that was all. He kept his lips pressed tightly together then, like he was fighting hard not to say anything.

Then the Feds called again.

There were three of them this time, including Jake. They waited downstairs in ominous silence until Nick was ready for them. Then they all came up to his lounge, refused cigarettes and drinks and wouldn't even sit down.

'Okay,' said Nick. 'What's on your mind?'

'Lola Gray,' said Jake. 'The dame that used to live here.'

Nick raised his eyebrows. 'Lola?' He shrugged. 'What about her?'

'She was fished out of the river twenty miles downstream,' said Jake, and the fury was trembling in his voice. 'Musta been in the river weeks. How come you didn't report her missing?'

'But, fellas,' said Nick smoothly, 'I haven't seen Lola for weeks. Not since she got mad and walked out on me.'

The Feds looked at each other. Jake said gruffly, with narrowed eyes: 'That's one more thing we're gonna get you for, Fenner. You big guys at the top figure you can jump the rap and leave the little guys to hold the bag. Well, it may have worked in the past. It may work in the future. But it's not gonna work all the time. Someday, Fenner, you're gonna …'

Nick said easily, 'You bore me, fellas. Haven't you got some other angle you can play up?'

'Yeah,' said Jake. 'We have. The new dame you've installed. We wanna see her.'

Nick lost his composure. His face became hard, kinda mottled. He said in a brittle voice: 'Now listen, you guys. You leave that dame outta this! If you worry her, I'll crucify you. If you start talking to her and ...'

'You'll crucify her,' mocked Jake. 'The same way Lola got crucified.'

Nick's clenched fists showed how hard he was trying to keep his temper in check. 'Get out of here!' he snarled. 'Get out of here!'

Jake said firmly: 'We wanna see that dame, Fenner. I wanna see her now. Here or down at headquarters.'

It was the Feds' lucky day. It was as though they whistled and got what they wanted. Sheila had been out shopping and chose that moment to walk into Nick's lounge. She hovered in the doorway, looked around with wide, startled eyes.

Nick said quickly: 'I'm busy, honey. Would you be good enough to leave us?'

'Of course, Nick ...' she began.

Jake interrupted, his voice steely and ringing with command: 'Just a moment, lady,' he called. 'We wanna talk to you. We're Federal agents.' As he spoke, he produced his badge from his wallet, held it so she could see the Government seal.

Sheila stared at Jake uncertainly, not sure what she should do.

'You leave us, honey,' said Nick. His voice was soft, the way it always was when he spoke to her.

'And I'm telling you to stay right here,' rasped Jake.

'Do what I say, honey,' Nick said gently.

'But, Nick,' she protested. 'If these gentlemen are from the police, I can't very well …'

Nick sighed. 'Okay,' he said. He got up and offered her his chair. 'But remember, honey,' he told her. 'These guys are looking for trouble. Be careful what you say. They'll twist your words, make you a liar.'

She settled herself comfortably in the chair, said smilingly: 'Don't be silly, Nick. The police wouldn't do anything like that.'

Maxie and Whitey stared. The Feds raised their eyebrows, only just managed to maintain their poker faces. Nick shrugged. 'Have it your own way, honey,' he sighed.

Sheila straightened her skirt demurely, clasped her hands on her lap, and looked straight at Jake. 'What is it you want to ask me?' she said innocently.

'How long you been around this joint?' he asked bluntly.

She thought. 'Just a few weeks,' she said.

'You look a nice dame,' he said.

She blushed.

'What's your position here?' he asked bluntly. 'You're his lay, aren't you? Get paid for services rendered? '

She stared at him, perplexed, didn't understand him.

He swallowed, repeated with emphasis: 'You're his mistress, aren't you?'

The scarlet spread upwards from her neck until her cheeks flamed. She was almost trembling with anger, her eyes flashing. 'How dare you!' she said.

If Jake had been standing, her reply would have rocked him back on his heels. He gaped, gulped. Then he eyed Nick apprehensively as Nick swayed over towards him, both fists bunched into hard knuckles.

'Take that back!' rasped Nick. 'Take it back or I'll knock it down your throat!'

Jake looked from him to Sheila. He swallowed some more, licked his lips. 'Listen, lady,' he said more softly. 'If I'm on the wrong angle, I'll take it back. But seeing the kinda company you keep, you can't blame me for drawing wrong conclusions.'

Sheila was still furious. 'And what's the matter with Nick?' she demanded. 'There's nothing wrong with him that I can see.'

'Of course not,' sneered Jake. 'There's nothing wrong with Nick. There's nothing wrong with prostitution, nothing wrong with gambling saloons, or crooked race meetings.' His eyes narrowed. 'There's nothing wrong with any of them, lady. And there's nothing wrong with killing, deliberate cold-blooded killing. You're in favour of all of them, I guess.'

He didn't ring any bells with Sheila. She looked at him like he was crazy. Then she looked at Nick as if he was a saviour. 'What's he talking about, Nick?' she asked. 'Why is he acting this way?'

'It's like I told you, baby,' said Nick. 'Cops are all the same. They've got swollen feet and swollen heads. You've seen the way they act, so now be a good girl, step outside and leave me to handle them.'

'I will, too,' said Sheila, flushed with indignation. She climbed to her feet, glared angrily. 'I don't see why I should stay here and be insulted.'

Maxie followed her to the door, closed it behind her. Jake looked at Nick. He said smoothly: 'Either that dame really doesn't know anything or she's a damned fine actress.'

Nick said levelly: 'She doesn't know anything, not a thing.' He kinda shrugged. 'I guess if she did, she wouldn't be here.'

Jake eyed him keenly. 'For a real hard case like you, it's interesting to see you getting soft about a dame.'

Nick snorted. 'I'm not interested in your opinions. If there's nothing else you want, you can go.'

Jake lounged to his feet slowly. 'I guess there's nothing else we want right now,' he said. He put his hands into his pockets, strolled across to the door. 'We'll be around again, though, Fenner. You might be uncertain about a lotta things. But you can be sure of that.'

'Maxie, Whitey,' ordered Nick crisply. 'Go downstairs and see these monkeys off the premises. Don't let 'em in again unless they've got a search warrant. D'you understand?'

Jake said: 'Don't worry, Fenner. The next time we come, we'll have that search warrant.'

Nick was sweating after they'd gone. He mopped his forehead with his handkerchief. 'Get me a drink, will ya, Joey?' he said.

I got him a drink, poured three fingers the way he liked and added just a splash of soda.

'The nerve of them guys!' he told me. 'Speaking to Sheila that way. I coulda killed them!'

'Feds always mean trouble,' I told him, remembering the very words he'd used himself.

'Yeah,' he said thoughtfully. He was wrapped up in himself, miles away.

'Sheila's pretty,' I said. 'I don't think it's right them Feds should talk to her that way.'

'You're right, Joey,' he said absently. 'You're right.'

'The police never did treat her proper,' I told him.

'That Bannister guy wasn't treating her right, either.'

'Sure, sure,' said Nick. He was still thinking.

'I was sure glad you knocked off that Bannister guy,' I told him. 'He had no right treating her that way, hurting her arm, squeezing it that way ...' I broke off.

There was a kinda tension. I could feel it in the room as distinctly as if it was a sharp splinter of ice that pierced from Nick to me. He was staring at me with eyes frozen in horrible intensity.

'What was that you said about Bannister, Joey?' His voice was so low I could hardly hear him.

'He's the cop,' I explained to Nick. 'He's the cop that got killed. You remember him. He's the guy that the Feds are worried about.'

I could see the veins standing out on his forehead. He was forcing himself to speak calmly, smoothly. His voice was nice. Just like black velvet. 'What did you say about Sheila and the cop?'

I wasn't sure now. I frowned, thought about it. Now I was thinking about it, my memory kept eluding me.

'Think, Joey,' urged Nick. 'You've gotta think, Joey. Try hard. You've got to!'

It was important to Nick. I'd do anything for Nick. I tried hard, and I remembered.

'The dame and Bannister,' I said excitedly. 'Bannister was the cop who arrested her. You remember, Nick. It was that night when ...'

It happened so quickly. I was up against the wall with Nick's hands twisted in my collar and choking me before I realised it. I tugged at my collar, half-choked as Nick squeezed it tighter.

'What are you trying to tell me?' he rasped frantically. 'That dame Sheila. Is she the dame Bannister arrested that night?'

I tried to suck in breath, managed it with difficulty, nodded and croaked: 'That's what I was trying to tell you, boss.'

His face was so contorted with anger, I thought he was gonna throw me across the room. He was shaking all over like he had the ague. Then slowly, ever so slowly, he calmed down. I hardly recognised his voice when he flared at me: 'Don't you realise what you've done by bringing her here? She was the one person in the world who knew we'd ever seen Bannister! Don't you realise what it means, Joey? She knows enough to have us all dangling at the end of a rope!'

I didn't understand half what he was saying. But I knew he was angry. Scared too. And it was something to do with Sheila. He was afraid of her.

I managed to work his fingers away from my neck. 'I'll do anything, boss,' I said. I was almost crying. 'I don't wanna get you mad like this. I'll do anything you want, anything to make you happy.'

He'd calmed down so much now, he was almost sagging. He walked across to the settee, sank down into it, buried his face in his hands. For a time, his shoulders shook like he was sobbing.

I went over to him, stood beside him, said humbly: 'I'll do anything you want, Nick. You just tell me. I'll do it.'

He looked up then. I'd made a mistake. He wasn't crying. But there was a kinda haunted indecision in his eyes. 'You poor sucker, Joey,' he said. 'You don't understand anything, do you? It happens all around you, and you only get half of it.'

'I understand a lot of things, boss,' I told him proudly.

'Look. Do you understand this, Joey?' He seemed terribly determined I should understand it, emphasised it again and again. 'You've got to understand this, Joey. You must never tell anyone what you've just told me. About Bannister and Sheila, I mean. You must never let Whitey know. You must never tell Maxie. Do you understand that? You must hang on to that thought, get it deep down in your head.'

'Sure, boss,' I said. 'I can do that.'

'Fine,' he said. 'Now keep thinking of what I've told you, Joey. Don't ever forget it.'

'No, boss. I won't forget it.'

He gnawed his thumb. I waited. He kept thinking. Finally he said: 'Go get her, Joey.'

'Who?'

He sighed. 'Sheila,' he said. 'Tell her I want her.'

She came readily enough, anxious to hear what had happened to the Feds. As soon as she was in the room she started. 'Nick. Who are those men? What right have they to ...'

'Forget them, honey,' he said. 'There's something more important; something we've gotta do right away.'

'What's that, Nick?'

'We're getting married, honey,' he said. 'We're getting married tonight.'

She stared at him, eyes wide and misty. 'Nick,' she said, like it was the happiest moment of her life, 'you don't really mean it? You really want to marry me?'

'Sure, honey,' he said. 'It's been on my mind all the time. I know now it's the thing I want more than anything else. And now I've made the decision, I just can't wait. Is it a go, honey?'

'Is it a go?' she repeated, her voice thrilling with excitement. 'Nick! How can you ask?'

Nick winked at me. 'You're standing on your foot, Joey,' he said. And this time he wasn't mad. He said it as a joke.

I gaped at him.

'Scram!' he said.

I looked at Sheila. Her eyes were sparkling, her mouth rippling with laughter. 'Nick means he wants you to leave us alone,' she explained.

'Okay, boss,' I said.

I wandered out glumly. It beat me. Why did dames always wanna be alone with guys? It just didn't make sense.

11

I was pleased Nick got married. It made him happy, and anything that made Nick happy made me happy too.

Sheila was happy also. You only had to look at her sparkling eyes, and see the tender look on her face when she looked at Nick, to know how happy she was.

None of us saw so much of Nick these days. Most of the time he spent going around with Sheila. Maxie and Whitey began to complain he wasn't paying enough attention to business. Business was getting more and more difficult, too. Collecting the takings became a weary job. All the guys we collected from beefed like hell about the way the papers were campaigning against vice, and the way the Feds were making themselves a nuisance.

The news-sheets said the Government were taking a stern view of conditions in our town. Another dozen Feds had arrived recently to widen the search for the murderer of Bannister. They didn't seem to be getting anywhere, and I figured they must be wasting their time, because a couple of them were hanging around outside the nightclub day and night, doing nothing except following Nick wherever he went.

Those Feds were determined to cause trouble, and finally they did. The newspapers came out with the news first. A little later, Nick's phone was ringing continuously and guys were calling.

Nick said it was serious. Washington had decided to hold a Congressional investigation into the affairs of our town. Imagine that! The whole of America to monkey with, and they had to choose our town!

Nick was angry. But he was quiet and efficient as he answered telephone calls, interviewed collectors; sent me, Maxie and Whitey around to all our usual agencies, telling them to drop everything.

'It's gonna cost us dough,' he told us. 'But everything's gonna stop right from now. Let them send their investigators. They won't find a thing. They can investigate to their heart's content, turn the town inside out. They won't find a thing and will have to give us a whitewash certificate. We'll lie low for a while and start up again later.'

A coupla days later, the Congressional committee arrived with an army of Government agents. They didn't scare anyone. You couldn't buy a numbers ticket in town if you wanted. Madame had a '*Private Hotel*' board stuck up outside her joint, and the girls were taking a well-earned holiday in Florida. The pool rooms along the main street were just pool rooms, and we had a coupla warehouses stuffed with one-arm bandits, oiled and greased and stacked ready for use at a later date.

There was still the nightclub. Nick claimed he ran that on the level. There were no worries there. And to celebrate the arrival of the Congressmen, Nick threw a dinner for all of us that evening in his own nightclub, even invited me.

It was a swell dinner, good food and good music.

Maybe I wasn't quite so happy as I could have been, on account Nick said I wasn't to drink champagne. But it was good, just the same. It was good just to see Sheila and Nick looking so happy.

And then, halfway through the dinner, everything changed. I have a way of knowing these things. I could tell there was tension in the air. They were talking about the Congressional enquiry, Nick making jokes about it. Sheila asked suddenly: 'I suppose all this started on account of that policeman that was killed?'

There was a kinda frozen silence. Nick said quickly: 'Have some more champagne.'

She accepted it, smiled prettily and added laughingly: 'I don't like policemen.'

Maxie said with feeling: 'Me neither.'

'I haven't had much to do with them,' said Sheila. 'There was that nasty man the other day, the Federal agent. He was dreadful. Then there was that other policeman. The one who was arresting me; the one you took me away from.'

There was a kinda paralysed silence. Nick said quickly: 'D'you want to dance, honey?'

Whitey asked, equally quickly: 'The cop we got you away from?' There was disbelief in his voice, and sudden realisation too.

'Surely you remember?' she said. 'He was taking me to the police station when Nick came along and stopped him.' She smiled at Nick gratefully. 'I think I fell in love with you right then, Nick,' she told him.

Nick's face was white. It took an effort to give her a reassuring smile, pat her hand.

Whitey said, in a kinda cracked voice: 'You remember that cop, Sheila?'

'I'll never forget it,' she told him. 'It was a dreadful

experience. I thought I'd die.'

Whitey asked cunningly: 'Have you seen him around lately?'

'I never want to see him again,' she shuddered. 'Once was enough.'

Whitey persisted: 'Would you recognise him again if you saw him? Saw a photograph of him, for example?'

'I expect so,' she said. 'It wouldn't be easy to forget him.' Then she crinkled her brow. 'Why all this interest?'

Whitey sat back in his chair, gave his mean, twisted grin. 'Nothing to it,' he drawled. 'Just idle curiosity.' But when she wasn't looking, he gave Nick a glance that was evil and calculating.

From that time onwards, there was tension in the atmosphere. It spoiled the party. It made me unhappy. Then, when the cabaret was finished and we all went upstairs to bed, Whitey grabbed me by the shoulder, rasped into my ear: 'I wanna see you, Joey.'

Nick said goodnight, escorted Sheila into his apartment. The rest of us walked to our rooms further along the corridor.

Whitey bundled me into his room, Maxie followed behind. Whitey snarled at me: 'Did you know about that?'

'About what?'

'Don't play dumb!' he rasped.

Maxie interjected: 'Let me handle this.'

I liked the way Maxie spoke then. It was soft and gentle.

Maxie said: 'Did you know Sheila was the dame Bannister arrested?'

I thought about it. I wasn't sure. 'I think so,' I said cautiously. Then I remembered Nick had told me I wasn't to say anything about it. I tried to gulp back the words. 'No,' I said. 'I didn't know. She didn't know Bannister. I know she didn't know Bannister. She wasn't the dame Bannister was arresting. I remember it all now. She wasn't the one at all.'

Maxie looked at Whitey meaningfully. 'Nick knew about it all the time,' he said. 'He musta known. He's warned dumbo to keep quiet about it.'

Whitey said, with a rasp of hatred in his voice: 'I wanna talk to that guy.'

'You can talk to me right now,' said Nick from behind us. He'd opened the door quietly just as Whitey spoke. In the silence that followed, he closed the door, leaned his shoulders against it. 'Well?' he asked. 'Who's gonna start?'

Whitey got to his feet. He said angrily: 'That dame knows about Bannister. She knows we were the last to see him. She can hang us. Are you crazy or something, Nick? Don't you know you're putting our heads in a noose?'

Nick said easily: 'You guys don't think. Of course, I knew about her. Why d'you think I married her?'

There was a long silence. Maxie asked cautiously: 'You married her. So what?'

'Use your brain,' said Nick. 'A wife can't give evidence against her husband in a court. You oughta know that. No wife is obliged to give testimony against her husband.'

Whitey roared loudly: 'She's not married to me. It's you she's married to. Me and Maxie are wide open.'

Nick said quietly: 'I was the guy who killed Bannister.'

Maxie roared: 'They'll hang it on all of us. We were accessories. We were in it together. The dame saw all of us that night. She might not give testimony against you,

Nick. But she'll give testimony against us. She's that kinda dame. She's so honest, she's too good to live.'

Nick was looking cool and unperturbed. But I knew he was worried, could sense the anxiety, frustration and fear inside him. 'You guys have gotta see this the right way,' he said. 'She ain't gonna cause us no trouble. You can rely on me for that.'

Whitey said harshly: 'I rely on no-one when my neck's at stake.'

'I'll take her away,' said Nick. 'I'll take her away some other State. You won't have anything to worry about.'

Maxie demanded angrily: 'Are you going crazy, Nick? There's just that dame between us and the chair. After what we've been through together, d'ya mean to say you're gonna let a dame hold our lives in the palm of her hand?'

Nick was worried now. Desperately worried. 'Look, fellas,' he said. 'We've been together a long time. We've made a good thing of it. Let's call it a day now. You can have the nightclub. We'll split the dough. I'll clear out, take the dame with me.'

Whitey edged over alongside Nick. 'You're nuts about that dame,' he accused. 'You've gone crazy. You can't even think straight anymore.' He took a deep breath, added with significance: 'But we can still think straight. And we're telling you, Nick. That dame's too dangerous. Something's gotta be done about her.'

The fear was in Nick's eyes. Not fear for himself, but fear for Sheila. 'Now wait a minute, fellas,' he begged. 'We can find a way out of this.'

'Sure we can,' said Maxie ominously. 'I've already figured one.'

Nick looked at him hopefully. 'What's your idea?'

Maxie said slowly: 'There's a coupla Feds outside. They're on our tail all the time. So what's done has to be done with their knowledge.' He paused, looked towards me meaningfully. 'What's the matter, Joey?' he asked. 'Aren't your ears working properly?'

'Sure,' I said. 'I can hear what you say.'

Maxie's eyes returned to Nick's, slowly, meaningfully. 'We've always known we might want to use him for the last time. This is it. It's a pity, but it's gotta be done. It's gonna save our necks. The Feds can follow us. Dumbo can blow his top and the dame doesn't talk anymore.'

Nick's face was white as he listened. I didn't know if he could make sense of what Maxie said. I couldn't. But I sensed it had something to do with me.

'Sure, Nick,' urged Whitey. 'That's the way to do it. Straight and clean. The Feds will be trailing us, and they'll see it happen. They may have their suspicions about Lola. But they can't prove anything. This way, you'll be right in the clear, and the Feds will be eye-witnesses.'

I've never seen such a desperate look as that in Nick's eyes. He swallowed uneasily, faltered weakly: 'I'd like to think about it, fellas.'

'There's nothing to think about,' said Maxie easily. 'It solves everything. There ain't no other way.'

'I'd like to think about it,' repeated Nick huskily.

Whitey's eyes narrowed. 'There's gonna be no more thinking. Nick,' he said 'That dame's hot. The Feds are liable to get working on her at any time. Even if she wanted, she couldn't keep quiet. And she's not the kinda dame to wanna keep quiet. She'd shoot her mouth off under pressure.'

Nick pleaded: 'Let it sweat awhile, fellas. Let it

sweat ...'

Maxie said with savage menace in his voice: 'It's not gonna sweat, Nick. It's gotta be done. And it's gotta be done now. Go get the Judy, rouse her out of bed, tell her we've got a little trip to take.'

I could see Nick wanted to fight against them. But there was nothing he could do. Maxie and Whitey were determined.

Nick's shoulders drooped. 'Okay, fellas,' he said. 'I'll go get her.'

Sheila was irritable at being got up out of bed again. She was sleepy, too. We climbed into the car, Maxie driving. Whitey looked out through the back window. I knew what he was watching for. I looked myself, and saw the two Feds signal a waiting police car, climb into it and follow along behind.

The streets were deserted at this hour of the morning. Maxie said he knew of a little place that was just right for us. It would still be open.

Sheila said she didn't know why we had to get up in the middle of the night when we could have gone there any time.

Nick said there was an important customer we had to meet.

Whitey pulled a flask from his hip pocket, handed it across to me. 'Take a slug of this, Joey,' he invited.

I looked hopefully at Nick.

He said, tonelessly: 'It's up to you, Joey. If you want it, you have it.'

I wanted it and I had it. While I drank, Whitey was pressed up close against me. He kept moving around. Looking back on it, I guess he was trying to get my gun.

I didn't notice it then, though.

It was a dowdy little bar in the centre of town, with an all-night licence. When Maxie pulled into the kerb, the police car pulled up on the opposite side of the road. We stumbled down the steep steps to the basement, and a few moments after we got inside, the two Feds sauntered in, sat at the far end of the room and ordered beer.

Nick, Maxie and Whitey had beer. Sheila said she didn't want anything except lemonade, and, without asking me, Whitey bought me another whisky. It sure was good. It warmed me right down to my toes. I felt my blood getting hotter and hotter, beginning to boil until it was molten and tight in my brain.

Whitey said: 'Better get it over.'

Nick said quickly: 'Wait a minute. Hold it.'

He crossed over to Sheila, took her hand. 'Listen, honey,' he said. Then he broke off.

They stood that way for maybe a minute or so, looking into each other's eyes. Nick had that kinda holy look again, like he wanted to be tender and loving. She stared at him and as though she sensed something was wrong. She clutched his hand, held it tightly. 'Something's wrong, Nick,' she said. 'You're trembling. Something's wrong.'

'There's nothing wrong, honey,' he soothed. 'There's nothing wrong. It's just that I want you to know …' He broke off, licked his lips.

'Yes, Nick?' she said wistfully.

He looked at Whitey, he looked at Maxie. He scowled as though wishing them to hell. Then he said, slowly and deliberately: 'I want you to know that I love you, honey. I want you to know that maybe I haven't been all I coulda been. But there's been one good thing in my life. That was you. I want you to remember that, honey.'

She was staring at him, wide-eyed. 'There's something the matter, Nick,' she said urgently, worried. 'There's something wrong.'

'There's nothing wrong, honey,' he told her soothingly. 'There's nothing wrong at all.'

Whitey was watching with a sneering, contemptuous twist to his lips. Nick looked at him meaningfully, and Whitey said to me: 'You drunk that whisky yet, dope?'

'Sure,' I said. 'It was fine. It made me feel good inside and …'

'You dumb-bell!' he sneered. 'You big dope! You dummy!'

It was starting again, the hammering in my head and the red mist rising before my eyes.

'You dummy!' jeered Maxie. 'You great dope! Joey, the great dumb dope!'

It was happening. I couldn't stop it. The sweat springing out on me, drenching me through and through, and that great fear leaping inside me like a great shadow, paralysing me with its impact, making me shudder with the awful fear that I'd been robbed of it. I stood there, trembling, sweating, and the hammering echoing in my brain. Then it snapped. It had to snap. The paralysis melted from my limbs, and I dived frantically for the revolver, afraid it wasn't there, scared I was gonna die on account it wasn't there.

The relief was wonderful as my hand closed around the butt. I drew it out, quickly and swiftly.

'The dame,' yelled Whitey warningly. 'Watch out for the dame.'

His words echoed and hammered in my head. '*The*

dame. The dame. The dame.'

I got my revolver lined up, her eyes between the sights and the fear in her eyes making me feel wonderful, making me feel I was master of the world. I asked quickly: 'Can I kill him now, boss?'

I wasn't looking at Nick. Yet I could see him in my mind. He was standing there, white-faced, trembling and licking his lips, trying to find the strength to say something.

'Sure you can,' said Maxie. 'Sure you can.'

I didn't take any notice of Maxie. It was Nick I depended upon. 'Can I kill him now, boss?' I asked pleadingly.

As he spoke, there was a swift decision in his voice and command: 'Look at me, Joey,' he ordered. 'Look at *me*. Look at *me*, I tell you! Damn it, Joey, look at *me*.'

I had to look at him. It meant swivelling the gun sights away from her face. Nick's brown eyes stared at me levelly. I could see his forehead lined up between the sights. There was that wonderful feeling of exultation inside me. I had only to press the trigger and I should be fulfilled.

'Can I kill him now, boss?' I pleaded.

There was a long pause. It was an exceptionally long pause.

Then Nick spoke, and his voice was soft and smooth as it always was, giving me that wonderful feeling of pleasure and warmth. It was like black velvet, rich and wonderful.

'Me first, Joey,' he said. 'Then Whitey and Maxie. You can shoot now.'

I know things other people don't know. Even though I wasn't looking at the Feds behind me, I knew they were on their feet, rushing towards me. One of them was pulling a gun from his pocket as I pulled the trigger.

It was strange. I didn't get that wonderful feeling of exultation after all. Instead, as the red hole appeared between Nick's eyes and his head smashed backwards, there was sudden intense grief and a terrible sense of loss. It was so intense, I wanted to scream aloud as the gun bucked again in my hand and Whitey's mean lips parted in an agonised roar of pain.

A split second later, another shot rang out from behind me. Something hammered into my side, knocked me sideways, threw me across the room. I found myself lying on the floor with sawdust in my nostrils, a red mist before my eyes, that intolerable hammering in my head and pain burning deep down inside me.

The red mist was getting darker and darker. The darker it got, the better I liked it. I waded into it, so that it enveloped me completely. It was black then. Rich, peaceful, smooth and black.

Black velvet, like Nick's voice.

EPILOGUE

They were gathered around me, lots of faces all staring down at me. The guy who was nearest looked at his notebook and, in a business-like voice, asked: 'Is there anything else you can remember? Is that everything?'

'Sure,' I croaked. 'That's everything.' I'd been talking a long time. It had taken a lot of my strength, and my voice was dry.

'Sign here,' said the guy with the notebook.

I signed. They had to guide my hand, because I hadn't the strength.

'I wanna drink,' I said.

Two of the guys had white coats. One was holding my wrist, the other was staring straight into my face. The one staring straight into my face shook his head slowly. 'It won't do no good, fella,' he said. 'Drinking will make it worse.'

'What will be worse?' I asked. Something was going wrong with my eyes. Everything was so swimmy.

'The pain,' he said softly. 'Drinking will make the pain worse.'

He was crazy, didn't know what he was talking about. 'I've got no pain,' I told him. There must have been something wrong with his hearing, because he had to lean close to catch the words. I repeated them. 'I haven't got any pain.'

The guy in the white jacket shrugged his shoulders, said loudly, 'Queer thing that. Bullet in the head has affected his nerve impulses. He's not getting any pain reaction. Peculiar what a head injury can do.'

'I wanna drink,' I croaked.

'Let the poor devil have a drink,' said somebody.

The guy with the white jacket looked doubtful. Then he shrugged. 'Might as well. It won't make any difference, anyway. He musta used himself up. I don't know how he had the strength to go on talking like that.'

In a dim kinda way, I understood then what had been happening. It was all written down. All that had happened to me, all recorded on paper.

Somebody held my head, somebody held a drinking cup to my lips. It wasn't any good. The whisky didn't make me any less thirsty. It ran down my throat like beads of mercury rolling across a dusty floor. No moisture, no soothing quality.

No soothing quality! A great sob rolled up from inside me. Without knowing how, I knew I'd lost the one important thing in my life.

There was no more Nick!

I would never again hear his soft, soothing voice telling me to take it easy. There was a great hole where my heart had been. The world was empty, and I was full of misery. There could never be happiness for me again. Only this unbearable loneliness and intolerable misery. I wanted Nick. I needed Nick. I wanted him and he could never soothe me again.

'He's crying,' said somebody.

Imagine that! Somebody else feeling sad, too,

crying the way I wanted to cry. Jeepers, I needed Nick! The words choked in my throat. 'Nick,' I pleaded, 'I want Nick!'

They were bending over close to me. 'He is asking for somebody,' a voice said.

'Nick,' I croaked. 'I want Nick.'

'Can you beat that?' somebody said. 'The guy's crying for the fella he bumped off.'

The white-jacketed guy said softly: 'Leave him alone. He's not himself. Hasn't been for a long while. He's not got long ...' His voice tailed off before I could hear what it was I hadn't got long to do.

'About that dame,' said a different voice. 'She still keeps asking. We've got all we want from her now. Shall we let her see him – get it over with?'

There was confusion, people moving around, faces swooping down, looming large, peering into my face and receding rapidly.

Suddenly one of the faces was hers; soft, tender eyes filled with tears. Her soft voice said: 'Joey, Joey! Look at me, Joey!'

'I want Big Nick,' I croaked.

'Joey!' she said again, and all her voice was a sob.

I felt warmed and comforted. It wasn't like it was with Big Nick, a warm softness inside me that swelled whenever he spoke to me, making me feel good through and through. It was not the same. But it helped.

'Say it again,' I whispered.

'Joey,' she whispered with a break in her voice.

I could see the tears streaming down her face. But the softness of her voice warmed me so that I was almost happy.

'Say it again,' I pleaded. 'Say it again, say it again.'

'Joey,' she said.

'You'd better go now,' a voice whispered softly. 'He's going to sleep.'

'The dopes!' I thought vaguely. 'The dumbbells! They think I'm sleeping!'

I closed my eyes. I felt good now. It was crazy to talk about being in pain. Why should I feel pain? I wasn't worried any more. I knew Nick was gonna be around. I'd had a bad dream, thought I'd lost him. But that was crazy. Nick and me was gonna be around together quite a deal.

ALSO AVAILABLE FROM TELOS PUBLISHING

CRIME

PRISCILLA MASTERS
WINDING UP THE SERPENT
CATCH THE FALLEN SPARROW
A WREATH FOR MY SISTER
AND NONE SHALL SLEEP
EMBROIDERING SHROUDS
SCARING CROWS

MIKE RIPLEY
JUST ANOTHER ANGEL
ANGEL TOUCH
ANGEL HUNT
ANGEL ON THE INSIDE
ANGEL CONFIDENTIAL
ANGEL CITY
ANGELS IN ARMS
FAMILY OF ANGELS
BOOTLEGGED ANGEL
THAT ANGEL LOOK
ANGEL UNDERGROUND
LIGHTS, CAMERA, ANGEL

HELEN MCCABE
PIPER
THE PIERCING

ANDREW HOOK
THE IMMORTALISTS
CHURCH OF WIRE

Printed in Great Britain
by Amazon.co.uk, Ltd.,
Marston Gate.